24

A

Bomb Alert

Adventures on the Santa Lucia
Bomb Alert

Pamela Oldfield

For John –

Pamela Oldfield

An Armada Original

Bomb Alert was first published in Armada in 1989

Armada is an imprint of the Children's Division,
part of the Collins Publishing Group,
8 Grafton Street, London W1X 3LA

Copyright © 1989 Pamela Oldfield

Printed and bound in Great Britain by
William Collins Sons & Co. Ltd, Glasgow

One

Jay pushed past his sister and cried triumphantly "First in!" He dumped his duffel bag on the floor and threw himself on to the bed. Then he crossed his legs and arranged his arms comfortably behind his head. He had dark curly hair and the eyes behind his glasses were large and brown and full of mischief.

"Who cares?" said Ann. "Really, you are a baby sometimes. Nobody would think you were nearly ten."

Jay thrust a thumb into each of his ears and waggled his fingers.

"Very funny!" said Ann in a voice which suggested that it was not funny at all.

But she was not really cross because she knew her brother's silly behaviour was simply his way of hiding his excitement. Although they had travelled on the *Santa Lucia* many times before, arriving on board and settling in to the cabin was always a special thrill for both of them.

She began to unpack her clothes and lay them neatly in the drawer below the dressing table which separated the two beds. Her brown hair was very short and her grey eyes were serious. Jay, (short for Jason), began to read aloud from the ship's newsletter which had been left on the dressing table. This leaflet gave the passengers details of the various activities being offered to them during the five day voyage which would carry them from New York to Southampton.

She hung her one dress in the narrow wardrobe and pushed the empty duffel bag under her bed.

"That's me done," she announced smugly.

"Wow!" cried Jay. "Guess who the group is this time?"

"Give up," said Ann.

"Foxy Fanfare!"

"Never heard of them," she teased although, of course, she had.

The group was very popular and had been touring Australia and America for the past six months.

Jay pulled a face and said, "You must have heard of Foxy Fanfare!"

"No," she told him, "and I don't want to. Foxy Fanfare! What a ridiculous name."

"It's because of her hair," Jay explained. "The singer has red hair like a fox." He read on. "There's a good film on tomorrow – *Ghostbusters*."

"You've seen it," she said.

"I can see it again, can't I?"

Ann grinned to herself. Jay always intended to avail himself of the entertainment offered but never did, preferring to spend all his time in the room devoted to video games. Reluctantly he slid from the bed and began to unpack his bag, tossing his clothes higgledy-piggledy into the drawer.

"Why have we got a different cabin on this trip?" he demanded suddenly. "We're always on F deck. I like F deck."

"Dad left if a bit late," Ann told him. "By the time he booked, our cabin had gone to someone else. Anyway, what does it matter? They're all the same," Ann told him. "This cabin looks exactly like the one we usually have."

"It looks the same but it isn't the same," Jay insisted. "We're higher up the ship. If we get bad weather we'll roll about more."

"I thought you liked being rolled about. When we hit that hurricane last year you said it was the best trip we'd ever had! Anyway, this is E so we're only up one deck." She went through into the bathroom and arranged her flannel and toothbrush above the handbasin.

Mention of the hurricane had reminded her of the nightmare journey she would rather forget and she hoped that this trip would prove less eventful.

Ann and Jay were the children of Art Burnside, a famous cookery expert. Art was an American and Sally, their mother, was English. They were now divorced, however, and the children lived with their father in his flat in New York where they went to school. Since the divorce Sally had met and married an architect whose name was Gordon.

7

Since he was English they had made their home in England. Art Burnside travelled all over the world to collect recipes for his books and he made these trips during the children's school holidays. Ann and Jay spent their holidays in Hastings with Sally and Gordon. Art Burnside's brother had been killed in an air crash so their father insisted that they travelled to and from England on the liner. Today they were on their way to England for the Easter holidays.

Ann picked up the ship's newsletter and began to read where Jay had left off.

"Did you see that Bob Stuart is organizing a treasure hunt?" she asked.

Bob Stuart was the ship's entertainments manager.

Jay's eyes gleamed. "A treasure hunt! That's a new idea. I wonder what the treasure will be?"

"I don't know," said Ann, "but don't get too excited. It won't be the Crown Jewels!"

At that moment there was a knock on the door and a man looked in. He was about forty with a cheerful round face and an immaculate uniform.

"So, I've got the pleasure of your company on my deck this trip, have I?" he grinned. "Well, welcome aboard the *Santa Lucia* for the umpteenth time! I hope you'll both have a pleasant journey."

The room steward told them his name was Andrew Starke and he promised to be on hand if they needed him for any reason.

"Just ring the bell," he told them. "You know the ropes by now."

8

When he had gone Ann said, "I'm going up on deck to watch the rest of the passengers come aboard. Then later I shall go to the lido for tea at four o'clock."

"Pig!" said Jay amiably.

She laughed. "And where will *you* be at four?" she asked.

"The lido, of course!" he grinned. "I'm not daft!" The lido was an area which surrounded one of the ship's two swimming pools. At the poolside there were comfortable loungers for those who wanted to relax in the sun and further out, tables and chairs. Every day tea and cream cakes were served and today it was very crowded. Most of the tables were occupied so Ann was not too surprised when a youngish man approached her.

"May I share your table?" he asked her.

Ann detected a foreign accent and thought he might be French.

"Of course," she said.

He was smartly dressed in white slacks and an expensive-looking polo necked jumper. Ann thought he looked slightly hot and flustered and wondered if he was uncomfortable in his jumper. Although it was only April the sun was very warm and the lido's transparent domed roof protected the passengers from the cool breeze which blew from the east.

He introduced himself as Julio Benenzo.

"I come from Sorrento," he told her. "You know Italy? Eez very beautiful country."

"I've never been there," said Ann.

"Sorrento eez very beautiful town. Molto sea and sky, but many tourists come Sorrento in summer. In summer too crowded. In winter, eez better. You understand?"

"Yes."

"You are alone?" he asked.

"No. I'm travelling with my brother."

She looked round for Jay but there was no sign of him and shook her head at the waiter who offered her a second cream doughnut.

"I shan't be able to eat any dinner," she told him. Julio, it seemed, had no such scruples and he was soon tucking into his third doughnut! Ann had never seen an adult eat so fast. He seemed genuinely hungry.

After a little more conversation about Sorrento, he told her he had a letter to write and she watched him weave his way hurriedly between the crowded tables.

Almost immediately Jay appeared and threw himself down onto the seat that Julio had just vacated.

The waiter brought him a cup of tea and a doughnut and for a moment Jay ate in silence.

Then he said, "I went to the wrong cabin! I forgot we are on E deck. There were two men in our cabin."

"It's not our cabin," Ann protested. "It's just the one we usually have."

"The door wasn't locked," said Jay.

As he bit into the doughnut a large blob of cream fell onto his jeans.

"Mucky pup!" said Ann.

Jay scooped it up with his finger and ate it with exaggerated relish.

"What did they say?" asked Ann.

"Who?"

"The two men – when you went barging into the room?"

Jay put the last of the doughnut into his mouth and looked hopefully at the waiter.

"They weren't very pleased," he said with a slight shrug. "I think they were making a bomb."

Two

"A bomb?" said Ann. "Oh, honestly Jay. Pull the other leg – it's got bells on!"

"What do you mean?" He looked up innocently.

"I mean, I'm not that stupid, dummy!"

Jay shrugged again.

"Did they say anything to you?" she asked. "Did you apologize?"

"One of them said 'What the Hell!' and the other one said 'Get that kid out of here.'"

The waiter gave him another doughnut and he bit into it almost as eagerly as Julio had done.

"You've got sugar all round your mouth," Ann told him.

"So have you!"

Ann found a handkerchief and hastily wiped her face but by that time Jay was giggling with delight and she saw that there were no traces of sugar on her handkerchief.

"They'd got all the stuff spread out on the table," he went on. "Bits of curly wire and a clock and a bag of plastic explosive."

"Don't tell me," said Ann sarcastically. "They

were wearing masks and carrying guns and they spoke with Russian accents! You watch too many movies!"

"The older man with the funny eye pushed me out and slammed the door. I put my ear to it and listened and I could hear them gabbling, but not in English. Then someone else came along the passage so I had to skedaddle."

"I expect they were mending the clock," said Ann.

"With plastic explosive?"

"Don't be ridiculous, Jay. It must have been something else – like putty for instance."

Jay snorted. "I suppose now you're going to say they were mending a broken window! What happened to the broken clock?" He stood up. "I'm off."

"Well, remember, Jay. It's E deck."

He nodded unconcernedly and went off leaving Ann to ponder his story. She told herself that his imagination had been working overtime and looking at the peaceful scene around her it was easy to convince herself. She decided to go to the library and find a good novel but as she stood up and pushed back her chair there was a grunt of pain from someone behind her and she spun round. A young woman with red hair was bending to rub her ankle, a grimace of pain on her face.

"Oh dear!" said Ann. "Did I push my chair into you? I'm terribly sorry."

The girl smiled wanly. She had a small oval

13

face and short red hair and she looked vaguely familiar.

"It's OK," she told Ann, straightening up. "It just caught my ankle. No bones broken."

"I should hope not!" said Ann.

"Am I too late for tea, do you think?"

"I don't think so."

As though by mutual agreement they both sat down at the table and regarded each other with interest. Ann saw a girl of perhaps sixteen or seventeen with friendly blue eyes. She looked desperately tired, however, and her face was very pale.

"They have cream doughnuts," Ann told her. "They're delicious."

The girl sighed. "Don't tempt me!" she said. "I'm not allowed cream cakes."

Ann opened her mouth to ask why but closed it again. It seemed rude to be too inquisitive. Perhaps she was suffering from an illness and was on a special diet.

The waiter brought a clean cup and saucer and poured tea from a bone china teapot.

"No milk or sugar, thank you," she told him.

Ann repressed a shudder. She liked milk and two spoonfuls of sugar.

"My name's Ann Burnside," she said.

For a moment the girl hesitated. Then she said, "Mine's Sharon Bridges."

They chatted for about ten minutes but Ann did most of the talking. She did learn, however, that Sharon was travelling with her brother Sam and boyfriend Mick and someone called Toddy. It was their first trip on the *Santa Lucia*.

"You'll love it!" Ann told her enthusiastically. "We've crossed dozens of times but we still look forward to it. Most of the crew know us by name now and for us it's like a home from home."

"It's really nice to talk to another girl," Sharon admitted. "I do like men but they can get awfully boring." She looked past Ann and groaned. "Oh dear! Here comes the most boring one now. Toddy is our manager."

Ann turned to see an older man approaching. He was nearly bald and his waistline had long since disappeared under a roll of fat. He looked extremely bad tempered and ignored Ann completely.

"I thought I told you to rest!" he said to Sharon. "Two hours sleep, I said. Minimum."

"I couldn't sleep," Sharon told him. "And you know I don't like taking those horrible sleeping pills."

"I don't care what you like and don't like!" he exclaimed sourly. "You look terrible and you need to rest. The tablets are quite harmless."

"You told me that about those other pills," she said bitterly, "and look what happened!"

Seeing Ann's confused expression Sharon said, "They were supposed to give me energy but they gave me a splitting headache instead. And they affected my vision. I was seeing double! It was so scary!"

"Only because you took too many," he replied.

"You told me to take four!" she retorted. "When I looked on the box the next day it said no more than two! I don't trust you, Toddy."

"Well, I want you to rest," he told her. "You'd better come back to your stateroom and at least lie down. If you won't take the sleeping pills I'll get the room steward to bring you a cup of hot milk. That'll help you sleep."

Ann said, "A spoonful of honey's good in milk. That helps you to sleep. It won't have any nasty side effects either."

Sharon said, "Thanks, I'll try it." With obvious reluctance she rose to her feet.

"I'll have to go," she told Ann. "But it's been fun talking to you. Perhaps we'll meet up again sometime."

"I hope so," said Ann.

She watched them go regretfully.

Just as they reached the door two teenage boys ran up to them and Ann saw with surprise that they carried autograph books. Sharon smiled at them and said something and took a pen from one of the boys but Toddy snatched it away and pushed Sharon through the door and out of sight. Disappointed, the boys returned to one of the tables.

The waiter beside Ann said to her, "You know who that is, don't you? That's Foxy of Foxy Fanfare. They're performing later tonight in the Lucia Grill Room."

"Foxy! Oh, of course!"

No wonder the girl had looked familiar.

"She looks so dreadfully tired," said Ann. "I felt sorry for her."

"Well, she would, wouldn't she. She's been touring for six months. All over Australia in all that terrible heat. Then America. It's non-stop. Exhausting. Rather her than me." He laughed. "I think I'll stick to being a waiter! Oh! Coming madam."

As he moved away to another table, Ann moved also. She found an empty lounger and stretched out on it. Wait until Jay knew that she had been talking to Foxy! He would be green with envy, she thought with a grin. Sometime she would have to introduce Jay and no doubt Foxy would give him an autograph. Being a famous pop star did not seem as glamorous as she had supposed. Presumably Foxy had to watch her figure and that was why she dared not eat a doughnut. And fancy having to have a manager. That miserable man told her when to sleep and when not to sleep.

"I'd hate it!" she said aloud.

With a frown she recalled what Sharon had said about the tablets Toddy had given her to give her energy and shook her head. Surely a manager should have her best interests at heart? He seemed quite heartless.

She made up her mind to attend the concert in the Lucia Grill Room later that evening and if she got the chance she would have another talk with Foxy.

A glance at her watch showed her that there was still time to go to the library and then have a quick swim before dinner.

As she made her way to the library she caught sight of Julio leaning on the ship's rail, apparently studying the foaming green water which streamed past the huge ship and broke in an ever-widening wake behind her.

It was easy to forget, thought Ann, that the *Santa Lucia* was a ship and not a luxury hotel and that they had left New York far behind and were already butting their way into the vast, cold wastes of the Atlantic Ocean.

Three

That evening Ann put on her dress and Jay wore long trousers, shirt and bow tie. He preferred to be casual but when occasion demanded it he could look very smart.

They made their way to the Lucia Grill Room in plenty of time so that they could choose seats near the stage. If they sat too far back Jay could not see over the heads of other people.

People drifted in and found seats and talked cheerfully while they waited for the show to start.

Ann had told Jay over dinner about her meeting with Foxy and he was duly armed with a new autograph book which he had bought at the ship's gift shop.

Promptly at nine fifteen the overhead lights dimmed and a man walked on to the stage. He was swarthy with dark hair and his black suit looked a little too small for him.

Jay said at once, "That's not Mr Stuart." The man rubbed his hands together nervously as he faced the waiting audience.

"Well now ladies and gentlemen," he began. "As

19

a certain young man has already noticed, I'm not Bob Stuart. My name's Harry Stapley. Now that's not the name you have in your newsletter so I'll quickly explain that the resident entertainments manager was unexpectedly detained in England and couldn't be with us so I have been engaged to take his place." Ann was puzzled by his manner. He sounded as though he was repeating lines which he had learned earlier. "But I know we're going to – er, to get along just fine and this will prove to be a very enjoyable trip for us all." He paused and someone in the audience began to clap but then stopped again when nobody else joined in. "So, ladies and gentlemen, we'll now get on with the show and – and, er – Oh yes! Are you in for a treat tonight! Comedy, magic, and, last but not least, a top class group fresh from their tour of Australia and the States. Yes, ladies and gentlemen, Foxy Fanfare are travelling with us this trip and have generously offered to perform one or two of their most popular numbers for us during each evening's entertainment. The younger people among us will already be familiar with their music. For the er – more mature passengers it will prove an unforgettable experience. Tonight we have it all! So – er –" He seemed to search his memory and his face brightened. "So sit back and enjoy the show. First, our young comedian who will have you rolling in the aisles." He threw out a hand dramatically. "Mr Danny Steggle!"

To a roll of drums a young man ran on from the

side of the stage. He wore a wig of yellow wool, a loud checked suit and huge floppy shoes. Jay giggled hopefully.

Unfortunately, Danny Steggle did not live up to appearances. His jokes were old and his delivery laboured. Jay leaned towards Ann and hissed loudly, "Even I know better jokes than that!" A man sitting behind them said "Ssh!" and Ann gave Jay a dig in the ribs to shut him up.

The so-called comedian was followed by Madame Pavlova, an elderly lady who wore a dress of turquoise satin and did very successful conjuring tricks with a tinkling laugh. Exchanted, Jay clapped enthusiastically and she smiled several times in his direction.

Then she said, "Now for my next trick I am going to need the help of someone in the audience. What about you, madam?" She smiled at an elderly lady who shook her head determinedly. Jay's hand shot up but she appeared not to see him.

"You perhaps, sir?" she asked a portly gentleman but he also declined.

Jay stood up and waved both his arms frantically and she turned towards him. "Ah! A volunteer at last," she said. "Please join me on the stage young man."

Ann grinned as Jay rushed forward and took his place beside Madame Pavlova. She shook hands with him and chatted to him, asking him his name and age and questions about his school and his holiday.

As she talked, she moved casually around him. Ann suddenly guessed what was coming and grinned to herself.

"And now," said Madame Pavlova, "I think we are running out of time. What is the time, Jay?"

Jay glanced at his wrist but his watch was missing.

"My watch!" he cried. "It's gone!" For a moment he was completely fooled and turned stricken eyes in Ann's direction. With a flourish, Madame Pavlova produced the watch from somewhere and Jay gasped with amazement as he took it from her. The audience clapped loudly and Jay grinned with delight. Madame Pavlova said, "But fancy coming on to the stage improperly dressed, young man. You really should have worn a tie."

Jay said, "Oh, but I am –" Then discovered that his bow tie was missing. When that, too, had been returned to him Madame Pavlova's act came to an end.

Jay returned triumphantly to his seat.

"Don't tell me!" begged Ann. "You're going to be a magician!"

After that Harry Stapley appeared once more.

"And now the moment you've all been waiting for," he intoned. "It is my – my er – pleasure, to introduce Foxy Fanfare so let's give them a big hand!"

Many of the people in the audience were elderly and had never heard of Foxy Fanfare but they applauded generously nonetheless. With an exciting swish the curtains swung open to reveal Foxy and two young men bathed in a pool of purple light. To Ann's relief Foxy, in a short white leather skirt and matching top, looked bright and cheerful. Ann assumed that the milk and honey had done the trick.

Without any introduction they broke into their first number, a song called "Jet Star Waiting". They were very professional. Sam, Foxy's brother, had the same red hair but he was tall and lanky. He fingered the strings of his guitar lovingly and from time to time he glanced at his sister and smiled. Ann thought him good-looking.

Mick, Foxy's boyfriend, crouched over his drums, playing them with a kind of fanaticism. His long hair flopped into his face, partly hiding his intense expression.

At the end of the number the applause was louder than before and Ann, catching Foxy's eye, gave her the "thumbs up" sign and was rewarded by a flashing smile.

Foxy then sang a ballad in the drowsy style that had made her famous; her eyes closed, her voice husky.

The group played one more number and then the curtains closed to loud applause and the entertainments manager appeared again to thank them and promise another good programme for the following night.

Most of the audience began to drift away but Ann sat on, hoping to see Foxy.

Beside her Jay was fidgeting, eager to be off.

"It's too late to go back to the games room," Ann told him before he could put the request into words.

"But it's only half past ten!" he protested, though without much conviction. His father had given strict orders about bedtime hours and Jay knew he would have to give in. He just wanted to make his sister's task as difficult as possible. He was very fond of her but the difference in their ages irked him. He had complained on many occasions that if he had been older than Ann he would have been much more reasonable about silly rules!

Ann said, "It's a shame about Bob Stuart. He was such fun. I wonder what happened?"

"He told us," said Jay. "He was 'unexpectedly detained' in England."

"I know that but what detained him? That's what I mean."

Jay shrugged. "Perhaps he was ill."

Ann said, "Then why didn't they tell us the reason?"

"It's not our business," said Jay reprovingly, but Ann let the remark pass.

"I just thought it was a bit odd," she said. "The way he told it. And he's not much good at the job is he? He doesn't talk naturally to the audience, the way Bob does. This man sounds –" She stopped, unable to find the exact word.

"Sounds what?" Jay demanded.

24

"I don't know. Odd in some way. As though he's really a plumber or something pretending to be an entertainments manager."

"He was in our old cabin," said Jay. "He's one of the bombers."

"Jay!" she gasped. "For heaven's sake stop saying that."

Jay said, "Well, he was! He was the one who said 'Get that kid out of here!'"

"He couldn't have been," said Ann. "He's a member of the crew, not one of the passengers. The crew have their own quarters. You must have mixed him up with someone else."

"I did not mix him up. It was him."

At that moment Foxy came towards them, smiling broadly. Mick was with her, his arm draped lightly around her shoulders. Ann cried, "You were terrific! Weren't they Jay?"

But Jay was suddenly and uncharacteristically tongue-tied in the presence of his heroes and he held out the autograph book without answering.

Foxy and Mick signed it and by that time Sam had arrived and Foxy made proper introductions.

Foxy and Mick chattered away but Sam seemed rather shy. He, too, signed the autograph book and then he smiled at Ann.

Ann was longing to strike up a conversation with him but could not think of anything to say.

Close to, his hair was more auburn than his sister's and he had nice grey eyes and lots of freckles.

Foxy said, "Let's all go to A deck. They have a late night buffet and I could eat a horse!"

"What will your manager say?" asked Ann, surprised.

Sam said, "Oh, we won't see him again tonight. He'll be in the casino, gambling away all the money he makes from us!"

Ann thought she detected a trace of bitterness in his voice.

Mick said, "He gets twenty percent of all we earn so he ought to be a wealthy man but he can't stop gambling."

Foxy nodded. "He's a compulsive gambler. It's like a disease with him," she said. "He's not even very successful. We once watched him lose over five hundred dollars in one night!"

Ann was relieved to hear that the unpleasant Toddy was not likely to appear and, after she had shepherded Jay back to the cabin and bed, she joined her new found friends on A deck.

Perhaps twenty or thirty people were sitting at the tables, having helped themselves from the elegant buffet laid out under the striped canopy. Ann took cold turkey, potato salad, a bread roll and butter and poured herself a glass of milk. The group had kept a place for her at their table and she joined them eagerly. As they talked, she learned that being pop stars was anything but glamorous. In fact it was very hard work.

"Hours and hours on the road between gigs,"

Sam told her. "Constantly packing and unpacking; getting on and off planes; no regular sleep—"

"Jet lag," said Mick. "When you fly round the world you keep finding yourself in different time zones. You leave Gatwick at ten o'clock at night and you fly for seven hours. So when you land it should be five o'clock in the morning. But it isn't. It's only midnight!"

"So you have a very long night!" said Ann.

"Right! Your body has to get used to sleeping at funny times and it makes you feel very odd."

"Plus Toddy seems determined to starve us to death!" put in Foxy. "He thinks we all have to look lean and hungry!"

Mick grinned. "That's easy!" he joked, "because most of the time that's exactly what we are."

At last Ann plucked up the courage to ask the question that had been uppermost in her mind. "Why on earth do you do it?"

They laughed.

Mick said, "I do it because playing drums is the thing I love best in the whole world."

Foxy said fondly, "Take away his drumsticks and he'd wither and die – like a plant without water."

Sam smiled. "I have plans for my share of the money."

Foxy nodded. "He's going to start a riding school," she said. "The biggest most successful school in England. But it will cost a lot of money. We just need to stay at the top long enough."

Sam grinned. "Foxy always said she would go round the world with her share but we've done so much travelling she's gone off the idea."

Foxy laughed and Ann was struck by how much younger and happier she looked when Toddy was not around.

"I'll think of something, don't worry," Foxy told him. "I might become a private detective or start a boutique or a dancing school."

"You can't dance!" cried Mick. "At least not quick steps and tangos and stuff."

"I could learn," she retorted. "Anyway, look who's talking! You've got two left feet!"

Mick laughed. "When my aunt was a girl she always wanted to own a sweetshop. No prizes for guessing why! When she grew up she did just that and within two weeks she hated the sight of sweets. There's a moral in there somewhere."

They all laughed.

"Don't get the wrong idea," Foxy told Ann, "I love Foxy Fanfare. It really has been fun apart from the hard work, but I know it won't last for ever. There are always new groups coming along to push the others out of number one. When that happens we've got to have something else to turn to."

"What about you, Sam?" Ann asked. "Why do you do it?"

He shrugged. "I don't know really. It's fun, I guess, but somehow it all just happened and here we are!"

Ann asked them how they had actually started in the pop music business and Foxy gave a scream of pretended horror and clutched her head dramatically.

"You mean you didn't see us on *Wogan*?" she demanded.

Ann had to admit that she had missed it.

"Well, he asked us the same question," said Foxy. "Sam had a guitar for his birthday when he was fourteen and he needed someone to sing along with him so he roped me in. I didn't even think I could sing."

"You can't!" teased Sam but she ignored him.

"We played once at a school concert for charity and Mick heard us and wanted to join."

Mick continued the story. "Then there were three of us. I was ambitious and talked them into going in for a local talent show. Toddy heard us and that was it."

Suddenly Foxy put a hand to her mouth and tried to smother a yawn but Ann saw it.

"You'd better get to bed," she advised. "You must be shattered."

Mick and Sam also confessed to the need for sleep and they said their goodnights and made their way back to their respective rooms.

Jay was already fast asleep and Ann slipped into her bed. She was certain that she would never sleep but it had been a long day and within minutes her eyes closed and she was dreaming.

Four

The next morning Ann persuaded Jay to join her for a swim and together they made their way to the lido. There a few early risers were already taking their morning exercise and Ann and Jay quickly joined them. Ann was determined to swim twenty five lengths and struck out with the breast stroke. Jay jumped in and out a few times and practised his crawl, but after twenty minutes he declared himself bored and, after dressing hurriedly, departed to the games room. Ann completed her twenty five lengths and then began to practise a racing plunge.

Suddenly Sam appeared at the side of the pool. He dived in to join her and surfaced, wiping the water from his eyes.

"Jay told me you'd be here," he said. "I thought you might like some company. The others are still sleeping."

Ann frowned. "You say Jay told you?"

"Yes. He was dodging around on the boat deck. Goodness knows what he was supposed to be doing."

Ann shook her head. "It beats me," she said. "I

thought he was going to the games room to play his beloved video games."

Sam grinned. "Never mind Jay," he said. "Do you feel like a race? First one to do five lengths?"

"Make it one length!" laughed Ann. "I've already done twenty five."

She was quite a good swimmer and although Sam won, it was only by a few yards. Tired and breathless they pulled themselves up onto the side of the pool to recover.

Ann was enjoying Sam's company but part of her mind was on Jay. It was so unlike him to be anywhere except the games room. And what exactly did Sam mean when he described him as "dodging about"?

When she asked him he looked surprised but said, "Oh you know. Creeping about and hiding behind things. As though he was shadowing someone. You know what boys are like at that age. They do weird things like that."

"But who was he following?" she asked. "Could you see?"

"I'm afraid not – but does it matter? He was probably having fun."

Ann sighed. "You don't know Jay the way I do," she said reluctantly. "If you don't mind, I think I'd better have a word with him before he gets himself into trouble."

She left Sam to his swim and went in search of her brother but before she found him she was hailed by one of the ship's officers.

"Miss Burnside!" he said. "The captain would like to have a word with you." He looked rather apologetic, Ann thought, and her heart sank.

"What has he done?" she asked.

The officer smiled reassuringly. "I don't know but I don't suppose it's anything too terrible."

Ann said, "I hope not," but she did not feel at all confident as she made her way towards the bridge. She knocked on the door of the captain's cabin a few moments later and the captain himself opened the door.

"I think you wanted to see me?" she said.

"Ah, Miss Burnside. Come in."

The captain had been in command of the giant liner for many years and Ann knew him quite well, but being summoned to his cabin was still a nerve-racking experience.

"Do sit down," he said kindly and waved a hand towards a chair.

Ann obeyed.

"It's about your brother," he began. "Of course, I am quite sure he means no harm – just childish high spirits – but I'm afraid I have had a complaint about him so naturally I must follow it up."

Ann sat silent, wondering what was coming next.

"It seems young Master Burnside has been annoying some of the passengers," the captain told her. "Two of them, to be precise. First, there's a Mr Ferenzo."

Ann echoed the unfamiliar name. "Ferenzo?"

He nodded. "It seems that your brother forced his way into the man's cabin and refused to leave."

Ann cried out, "Oh no! That's not how it happened. At least, not how I heard it."

The captain raised his eyebrows.

"I'm sorry," stammered Ann. "I don't mean to be rude but Jay told me about that incident. You see, he forgot we are on a different deck this trip and he went to our old cabin on F deck. The number is the same. The door was open and he was inside before he realized his mistake." She hesitated but then decided against telling the captain what Jay had said about the bomb. Things were bad enough already.

The captain looked at her doubtfully. "I really can't see why Mr Ferenzo should distort the truth," he said. "According to him he burst in and disturbed Mr Ferenzo who was working on some papers. When Mr Ferenzo asked him to leave he was insolent. But that isn't all, I'm afraid. Mr Stapley, the entertainments manager has just been in to complain that your brother keeps following him about and won't go away. It may be some sort of game to your brother, Miss Burnside, but Mr Stapley finds it very embarrassing and he is understandably annoyed."

"I'm terribly sorry," said Ann. "I'll have a word with Jay. I promise you it won't happen again."

"I'd be very grateful," said the captain. "I don't think there's any call for apologies as long as the nuisance comes to an end."

Ann nodded soberly. It would never do for her father to hear about Jay's behaviour. He only allowed them to travel unescorted because Ann was willing to supervise Jay.

The captain saw Ann to the door and closed it gently behind her.

Flushed and furious, Ann went in search of Jay. This time he had really gone too far, she told herself grimly. He was not in the games room or the library so she decided to go down to the cabin and see if he was there. The lift doors opened and she slipped in and found herself sharing the lift with the young man called Julio and an older man whose left eye was closed as though in a permanent wink. At once Jay's words came back to her about the two men in their old cabin. Could this be the man with the "funny eye" and, if so, what connection was there between him and Julio?

For the very first time it occurred to her to wonder seriously if Jay *had* seen something suspicious. Her thoughts raced. If he had disturbed two criminals they would naturally be annoyed. But would they dare to draw attention to themselves by going to the captain to make a formal complaint. It seemed extremely unlikely, she reflected.

Julio was scowling but she smiled at him and said brightly, "Hello again!"

The one-eyed man gave Julio a startled glance and muttered something in a low voice. He spoke in a foreign language which Ann did not recognize. Julio,

34

still scowling, nodded towards his companion. "This man eez my brother Alfredo," he told her. His translation of this did not please the other man. Although Ann could not understand a word they were saying, she could see by Julio's sullen expression that he was being reprimanded for something.

Something made her pursue the conversation. "I'm Ann Burnside," she said.

Julio appeared to translate this for the benefit of the one-eyed man who then nodded grudgingly in Ann's direction.

"I hear Sorrento is very beautiful," she said in the same bright voice. Just then the lift stopped and an elderly lady joined them in the lift.

"Deck D," she quavered and Ann pressed the appropriate button for her.

As they went down Ann persisted with Julio's brother.

"Molto beautiful," she said. "Er – Sorrento molto bella."

It was obvious that he had no idea what she was talking about but again Julio translated. Alfredo nodded.

The old lady said nervously, "I've never liked lifts. Never. I got trapped in one once with my mother. I was only four at the time but I can still remember how terrified I was. And I always think, suppose the light should fail!"

Julio and Alfredo ignored her but Ann said, "There's always an alarm button. See? It shows up red even in the dark. You press it to get help."

The lift stopped and the old lady said, "Is this D deck?"

"No," said Ann. She glanced at Julio and his brother, assuming that they had pre-set the lift for C deck before she got in. They returned her look blankly.

With a shrug, Ann pressed the button and the lift descended again. When it stopped Ann told the old lady, "This is your deck," and she left them.

A family of four then crowded in, laughing and chattering and there was no opportunity for Ann to speak with Julio or his brother again.

They were still in the lift when she reached her deck and stepped out. She walked back to her cabin looking very thoughtful. Sitting on her bed she stared at the wall and a cold shiver ran down her spine.

Julio had told her his name was Julio Berenzo with a "B" but he had said the one-eyed man was his brother. The captain had described the man in their old cabin as Mr Ferenzo. With an "F"! How could they be brothers if they had different names? And how could they not know their own name?

"Oh Jay!" she whispered.

Another thought occurred to her. If Julio was Italian as he had told her and "molto bella" meant "very beautiful", how was it that his brother Alfredo had not understood the phrase? And what about Harry Stapley?

"Oh goodness!" she groaned.

Jay had said that Harry Stapley was one of the men in their old cabin. That made three of them. Were they all brothers?

"No," she said aloud. "Because the entertainments manager's name was Stapley and he spoke English with a cockney accent."

At that moment Jay burst into the room. One look at Ann's face removed his smile. He looked at her guiltily.

"The captain sent for me," said Ann and proceeded to tell him what had happened.

She was thinking furiously, however, wondering if it was wise to tell him of her own suspicions. He was too young to be involved and she most certainly did not want him to take any risks. If she confided in him he might well ignore the captain's warning and continue to shadow Harry Stapley. He could end up in serious trouble.

Ann recalled only too vividly the nightmare she had endured on a previous voyage when Jay had disappeared. She did not want to go through that again. The less he knew the better, she decided.

"Whatever made you follow him?" she asked. "The poor man was very embarrassed to have you creeping about after him and I'm not surprised."

"He was carrying the bomb," said Jay. "At least, it might have been the bomb. It looked about the right size for a bomb."

"Jay! You don't even know what a bomb looks

like!" exclaimed Ann, although her heart was thumping. "You must forget all about bombs and stop making a nuisance of yourself. Do you understand?"

"He put it in the dressing-up box," said Jay. "I saw him."

The dressing-up box was a huge chest which contained various items of clothing which the passengers could use for the fancy dress party which was always held on the third night of each crossing.

Ann's thoughts whirled. Was it possible? Certainly no one would want to open the chest until Thursday. But the chest was never locked. Surely it was much too risky. Anyway, there was no bomb.

Or was there?

"Look, Jay," she said, hiding her anxiety with difficulty, "you must promise me that you will stay away from that man and from Harry Stapley. And Julio, too."

"Who's Julio?" said Jay. "I've never heard of a Julio. Is he one of the gang?"

Ann cursed inwardly, furious with herself for the slip. Jay was as sharp as a needle.

"Julio is a friend of Harry Stapley," she improvised hastily. "So leave them alone. *All* of them."

"But what if they blow up the ship?" he demanded.

"They won't!" She crossed her fingers behind her back and made up her mind to go back to the lido and confide in Sam.

Jay shrugged. "Can I go now?" he asked.

"You haven't promised and you know that Dad

said I'm in charge while we're on the *Santa Lucia*."

He appeared quite unconcerned. "I promise," he said.

Before she could say more he darted out of the door and she heard him running along the passage.

She sat undecided for a few moments mulling over all that she knew. It was all so unlikely. She could imagine the captain's face if she approached him with such a bizarre story.

No. She could not go to him unless she was satisfied that there really was a bomb.

"A bomb on the *Santa Lucia*!" she whispered.

A luxury liner with thousands of passengers and almost as many crew! It would be a major disaster.

For a moment she imagined an explosion ripping the ship apart; she saw people injured and dying; she heard the cries of help from people in the water as the ship went down. With a shudder, she rejected the terrible vision. Such a thing could not happen. It was unthinkable.

She left the cabin and began to look in all the places where she might find Sam. As she passed the dressing-up box she gave the lid a tug. Then another. Shocked, she stared at it with a growing suspicion. For the first time ever it was locked!

Five

When she got back to the pool there was no sign of Sam. She began to look for him but without any luck, and suddenly she saw Toddy hurrying along the deck. He looked distinctly bad tempered and Ann wondered if he had lost a lot of money in the casino.

"Good morning!" she said.

"Oh, it's you!" He gave her a sour look. "If you're looking for Foxy you won't find her. She's confined to her cabin this morning."

"Is she ill?"

He hesitated. "No – just not well."

"What about Mick?"

"He's not well either."

He made to push past her but she stared at him. Sam had said only that they were sleeping late. She caught hold of his arm.

"What's wrong with them?" she said. "They were perfectly OK last night."

"It's nothing," he told her brusquely. "A virus, that's all. Just forget them, can't you?"

"No, I can't," said Ann. "If they're ill they should see the ship's doctor."

"They aren't ill!" he cried.

"But you just said they had a virus!"

"The doctor has been to see them," he said. "Now stop poking your nose in where it's not wanted. Foxy Fanfare is my business. I'm their manager, remember. I'm responsible for their welfare. Totally and *solely* responsible. It's in their contract."

Ann thought of what she had learned of him from Foxy and was tempted to say exactly what she thought of his efforts. She thought better of it, however. At least she must hold her tongue until she had seen them again. This wretched man had the power to keep them apart and Ann did not underestimate him.

"I saw Sam earlier," she told him. "He didn't say they were ill. Sam was fine."

"Well, he's not fine now. It was very sudden."

Ann knew he was lying.

"I want to talk to Foxy," she told him, keeping her voice steady with difficulty.

"Well you can't."

"Then I'd like to send her a note."

Again he hesitated. "You can give it to me. I'll see that she gets it when she wakes up."

"Is she asleep then?"

"I told you she was exhausted."

"You didn't," snapped Ann. "You said she was unwell with a virus."

He glared at her. "I don't have to waste my time with the likes of you," he told her and he

41

strode away through the crowd and was lost to view.

Now Ann was really alarmed. Foxy's words came back to her: "You told me to take four tablets . . . the next day I read the box and it said no more than two . . . I don't trust you, Toddy . . ."

Were they really suffering from a virus or had he somehow drugged them?

"Don't be so ridiculous," she told herself. "Your imagination is running away with you."

Surely it was in Toddy's interest to keep them healthy. They must have commitments back in England and if they could not keep them they would earn no money and he would have nothing with which to gamble.

She thought about Sam. He had appeared in perfect health at the pool.

She made her way back to the lido, threw herself on to a vacant lounger and tried to forget her idea that Toddy was up to no good and that Foxy Fanfare were somehow at risk.

After a quarter of an hour of anguished thought she was no nearer knowing what to do next. She had relied on Sam's help but now, thanks to Toddy, his advice was denied her. Unless . . . She sat up suddenly. She would find out where Foxy Fanfare's cabins were and go to see for herself. As long as Toddy was out of the way – she must not risk meeting him again. He had not been going in the direction of the accommodation decks so perhaps this was her chance. Swinging her legs to the ground she half-ran along the corridors to the lift and pressed button B. She knew that most of the first class staterooms were on that deck.

She stepped out at B deck and hurried along the corridor to the steward's room. A young woman in a neat brown uniform answered her knock.

"I told Foxy I'd call in on her this morning," she lied. "But I forget which is her cabin. She did tell me."

To her dismay the stewardess shook her head regretfully.

"I'm afraid we have orders not to let the public bother any of them," she told Ann. "Pop stars are so vulnerable, you see. They are pestered day in, day out, by people who want to have their photograph taken with them. Or else they want autographs. They get no peace, poor things. We're just trying to ensure a little privacy for them. I'm sure you understand."

"I do understand," Ann told her, "but I'm not just a member of the public. I'm a special friend."

The stewardess hesitated. "I'll check your name on the list," she said and ducked back into the room and reappeared with a sheet of paper. "Mr Todd has given me a list of people who can be admitted. He takes his job very seriously, you see. Nothing is too much trouble. He's like a father to them. You're Miss Burnside, aren't you? I remember you from way back."

"I don't suppose I'll be on the list," said Ann.

"Foxy and I only really met yesterday. I don't suppose Mr Todd has had time to add my name to the list, but we really are friends."

The woman shook her head and folded the paper. "I'm sorry," she said. "If your name's not on here, it's more than my job's worth to let you in. Mr Todd would never forgive me."

Ann thanked her and walked away, frustrated but reluctant to give up the attempt. An idea came to her and she turned back.

"Could I have a sheet of notepaper then, and an envelope?" she asked. "Surely no one would object to a note. That's not an invasion of privacy, is it? I could just push it under her door."

To her intense relief the stewardess agreed and after a moment produced paper and envelope. Ann then had to ask for a biro and every second seemed an age. If only Toddy would stay away. Now Ann began to wonder how much she dared put in the note. Suppose Toddy found it. After much thought, she began to write in capital letters:

"DEAR FOXY. HOPE YOU ARE SOON RECOVERED FROM YOUR VIRUS. . ."

She underlined the word virus then continued.

"I WANT TO SEE YOU URGENTLY. . ."

Should she sign her name, she wondered, or could she think of a nickname that Foxy would recognize?

What about Anna Karenina? No, Foxy might dismiss it as a hoax. Perhaps she could make an anagram of her name – no, that would take too long and anyway, if it was too difficult Foxy might not be able to decode it. Unable to think of anything more subtle she finally signed it "J'S SISTER" and hoped Foxy would work it out.

The stewardess was waiting nearby and innocently Ann asked her the number of Foxy's cabin.

"Thirty two," she said, "but I'll give it to her, if you like."

She held her hand out but Ann was thinking desperately. Suppose Toddy asked if anyone had called to see them; the stewardess might mention the note – or worse, give it to him to deliver. She would not risk that.

"It's OK," she said briskly and set off in the other direction, checking the numbers as she went. Thirty four . . . thirty three . . . thirty two!

Stooping, Ann bent to push the note under the door. Glancing back she saw that the stewardess had gone and immediately she straightened up and banged on the door with the side of her fist.

"Foxy! It's me, Ann!" she called loudly. "Can you hear me? Can you answer me?"

Silence greeted all her efforts and at last she gave up.

Which was Sam's cabin, she wondered. Did he and Mick share a room? She looked at the door on either side of number thirty two but dared not knock in case she disturbed someone else. The captain would not appreciate any more complaints!

Six

Lunchtime came and still there was no sign of Foxy Fanfare. She began to feel really worried but reassured herself that they must appear at the concert that evening or questions would be asked.

She finished her meal and was making her way out of the dining room when she caught sight of the ship's doctor sitting at another table. He had finished eating and was drinking a cup of coffee and without giving herself time to think she hurried up to him.

"How are Foxy Fanfare?" she asked him. "Isn't it terrible? I could hardly believe it. Are they going to come round, doctor?"

He looked at her in astonishment. The man next to him said, "What's the matter with them?"

Ann rushed on. "Someone has just told me they're desperately ill. In a coma. Food poisoning or some such. Are they going to die, doctor?"

The doctor smiled and shook his head.

"Well, Miss Burnside, I don't know where you heard that crazy story," he laughed, "but I can assure you there is nothing wrong with them whatsoever. At least, not to my knowledge and, you know, I rather think I'd be the first to know."

They all laughed at this and Ann assumed an air of great relief.

"Then they're *not* ill?"

"Certainly not! Who told you that they were?"

"Oh er – someone I met at the lido," she invented. "I don't know his name."

One of the other diners laughed. "Shipboard rumours!" she said. "I think people get bored and then these stupid rumours go the rounds. I was on my way to India once many years ago and I remember someone telling my father that one of the passengers had fallen overboard. There was such a to-do! Of course it wasn't true at all, but it caused quite a commotion!"

The doctor patted Ann's arm. "Rest assured, young lady, Foxy Fanfare are alive and well and will live to fight another day!" They all laughed again and dutifully Ann joined in.

"I'm so glad," she said and left them to their coffee. But her face was grim as she tried to make sense of it. If Foxy Fanfare *were* ill the doctor certainly did not know it. If they were *not* ill then where were they? And why had Toddy lied?

She went on deck and leaned on the ship's rail, watching the water far below. Usually the sight had a calming effect but today proved the exception. Her head was spinning with half-formed ideas and deepening suspicions. Suddenly she whispered, "The dressing-up box!"

She would ask someone to unlock it!

But not Harry Stapley.

After a few moments consideration she thought of Marion Wells, Bob Stuart's assistant.

Marion was in the office, busy with a queue of passengers for the weather was not so good and the board games were in great demand.

"I don't want draughts," a woman was insisting. "I want halma."

"I'm afraid all the halma sets are out," Marion told her. "What about chess? I have a couple of—"

"Oh no! Not chess!" she cried peevishly. "I don't feel like concentrating today. And my nephew doesn't like chess because they have to play it at his school. He particularly asked for halma."

She went away disappointed and the next in the queue, a boy of about Jay's age, marched off with a game of Cluedo.

Marion smiled when she saw Ann. She was a plump, cheerful woman with curly black hair tied back with a bow.

"Miss Burnside!" she exclaimed. "Nice to see you again. What can I get for you today? Have you tried Trivial Pursuit? A real brain teaser that is and great fun. Or we've got Monopoly—"

Ann leaned forward so that she could lower her voice.

"Please could I have the key to the dressing-up

box?" she asked. "I've got a marvellous idea for the fancy dress party—"

"Oh, but it's not locked!" Marion looked at her in surprise. "It's never locked. Surely you know that."

"Well, it is now," Ann told her. "I tried it an hour or so ago and I couldn't open it."

Ann saw the disbelief in Marion's eyes.

"If I could just have the key –" she began but at that moment a voice behind her said, "The key to what?"

Harry Stapley was looking at them enquiringly.

"The key to the dressing-up box," Marion told him. "I was just telling Miss Burnside that we never lock it."

"And I tell you it's locked!" Ann insisted.

A variety of emotions flitted across Harry Stapley's face and Ann could have sworn that fear was one of them.

He glanced around him anxiously. "It's a bit premature to be worrying about a fancy dress costume," he told Ann. "You've got all day tomorrow. What's the hurry?"

"I want to make sure I get what I need," Ann invented. "I've got this marvellous idea—"

By this time another queue was forming and to Ann's embarrassment everyone seemed to be taking an interest in their conversation.

"Look, may I borrow the key or not?" she said, anxious now to force the issue. "Or are you going to pretend it's lost?"

Just for a second or two Harry Stapley's eyes glittered with an emotion Ann could not recognize. She only knew it frightened her.

"Now why should I pretend to have lost the key?" he demanded. "You really are becoming a little hysterical, Miss Burnside."

"I don't know why you should," said Ann, "but then you don't seem very keen to let me have it, do you?"

A voice behind her said suddenly, "Oh, dressing up is *such* fun! It always reminds me of Christmases long ago." Ann turned to see Madame Pavlova smiling at her. "When we were children we lived in a big house and had lots of servants and they used to dress up too."

Seizing her chance Ann told her. "There's a fancy dress party tomorrow night. Mr Stapley is just getting the key to the dressing-up box so that I can start my costume."

Unaware of the look on Harry Stapley's face Marion said, "Tomorrow is going to be a bit different. It's going to be a masked ball!"

Madame Pavlova clapped her hands. "Oh, how perfectly splendid!" She beamed at the discomfited entertainments manager. "I'll come along to the box with you," she said. "I once went to a party as –" She clapped a hand to her mouth and a diamond ring glittered, "– but I mustn't tell or else you'll know me even with the mask."

She looked expectantly from Marion to Harry

Stapley and it seemed to Ann that everyone waited.

She felt a ripple of fear. Suppose there was a bomb in the box and it was designed to go off when the lid was raised? Harry Stapley now began to bluster and fuss about the key, pretending to have mislaid it but by this time several more passengers decided that they would like to start on their costumes. Suddenly out of the corner of her eye, Ann saw a slim figure appear at the door and whirled round in time to see Julio give a brief nod of his head before disappearing once more onto the boat deck.

As Ann turned back she saw Harry Stapley's expression undergo a complete change. Gone was the hunted look as he smiled expansively. Thrusting his hand into the pocket of his jacket he said, "Ah, here it is after all. How silly of me. Well, let's see about this box, ladies and gentlemen."

He strode off, his step full of confidence, and everyone fell in behind him. Like the Pied Piper of Hamelin, thought Ann, with the rats following to their doom. She followed slowly behind him, piecing together in her mind what had happened. She knew now that there would be nothing in the box. Julio had seen to that. Whatever it was had been removed while Harry Stapley had kept them all at the desk, arguing. The nod from Julio had been a signal to Harry that all was clear.

So something had been in the chest. But no one would believe it was a bomb, just as no one would believe that Foxy Fanfare were in any kind of trouble. Toddy would be able to convince the doctor that they were fine and Ann would never be able to persuade anyone to force their way into Foxy's cabin.

As she reached the group round the dressing-up box, Harry Stapley bent down and tugged at the lid. It swung open without needing to be unlocked.

He turned mocking eyes in Ann's direction. "You see, Miss Burnside!" he said. "All that fuss for nothing. It was never locked."

The others began to rummage in the box and with another challenging smile at Ann, Harry Stapley left them to it.

Sick at heart, Ann leaned over the box, making a pretence of looking for something suitable. She pulled out a gold coloured cloak and draped it over her arm. Madame Pavlova was tugging out a long skirt made of blue velvet.

"Oh, how beautiful!" she exclaimed. "Now I need some silver paper but I won't tell you what for. That must be a secret." She smiled at Ann and said, "What is your name, dear? I saw you last night. You were sitting with my young assistant."

"I'm Ann Burnside," Ann told her distractedly.

"Ann Burnside," she repeated. "Thank you. And am I right in thinking that the young man is your brother?"

Ann nodded.

She felt helpless and alone. She wanted to tell

52

somebody her fears, but after Jay's escapades she could not face the captain. It seemed there was no one she could confide in.

"Excuse me," she said and with a faint smile she made her way slowly back to her cabin. Once inside, she threw down the cloak with a gesture of irritation and sat on the edge of her bed. The safety of the *Santa Lucia* rested in her hands. She had never felt so alone in her life!

Seven

A tap at the door made her jump and she sprang to her feet warily. It couldn't be Jay because he had a key. It might be one of the bombers and she was quite defenceless.

"Who is it?" she asked.

"It's me – Madame Pavlova," came the surprising reply. Quickly Ann opened the door and invited her unexpected visitor into the cabin.

Ann indicated Jay's bed and said, "Do sit down."

Madame Pavlova settled herself with fluttering movements of her delicate hands and Ann caught a distinct whiff of mothballs from the old fashioned pink dress she wore. She really was a rather extraordinary person, angular and fragile, and she reminded Ann of a flamingo. Her smile was sweet, however, and her fluffy white hair framed a face that had once been very beautiful. Her pale skin was fine and her faded blue eyes were large.

Ann wondered what she could possibly want – unless it was something to do with Jay. Perhaps she wanted to enlist him as a permanent partner in her act! The old lady's first words, however, promptly ut paid to that idea.

"It *was* locked," she told Ann. "The dressing-up box, I mean. Now why on earth should they lie about a thing like that? It's been puzzling me." Her sweet smile had gone and her eyes were shrewd as they looked at Ann. "Of course," she went on, "you can tell me it's not my affair and if you do I shall forget all about it. But I thought you looked a trifle upset and I'd like to help if I can."

For a moment Ann looked at her in silence. She longed to confide in someone but this frail old lady was hardly the person she would have chosen. At a guess Ann thought that she must be at least seventy years old – hardly the time of life to be getting mixed up in crime!

To gain a little time she asked, "When exactly did you try the lid of the chest?"

"Yesterday. I asked the young lady for the key and she said Mr Stapley had it."

There was a long silence while Ann tried to decide what to do and Madame Pavlova sat with her hands crossed demurely in her lap.

Suddenly the old lady said, "Are you afraid of something?"

Ann still hesitated.

"Someone, then?"

"Yes."

"And have you confided in anyone?"

"No. I don't think anyone will believe me." There were so many reasons, she told herself, why she

55

should not involve Madame Pavlova and yet he
instincts were to pour out the whole story. If only
she had been able to speak with Sam. He would
have believed her, she was sure.

"Do you think you are in any danger?"

The blue eyes fixed on hers were cool and cal
culating and Ann began to wonder if looks were
deceptive. Was Madame Pavlova as helpless as she
looked? Reluctantly, Ann said, "I think we all are."

"Then shouldn't you share what you know?"

"It's not quite as easy as that," Ann protested.

There was another silence and then Madame Pav
lova reached out and took hold of her hand. "Look
at it this way," she urged. "Suppose something hap
pened to you. All that you have learned of whatever
it is would be lost. Does that thought make it more
reasonable that you should confide in someone -
even an old dodderer like me?"

Ann felt herself blushing but Madame Pavlova
laughed kindly.

"Oh I have no illusions," she said, "but if i
makes you feel any better I have led a very tough
life and I'm one of the world's survivors."

Ann said, "If what I suspect is really happening
then telling you puts you in danger – and it all sound
so crazy that you may not believe me."

Madame Pavlova smiled. "You have come thi
far," she pointed out. "Why not tell me the rest?"

And Ann realized with a rush of gratitude that
by her skilful questions, the old lady had made the

56

decision for her. She certainly was not as helpless as she appeared!

"I'll tell you," she said and took a deep breath. Madame Pavlova's smile faded and her eyes narrowed as she listened.

Ann began haltingly with Jay's insistence that he had seen two men making a bomb. She went on more confidently to describe her various encounters with Julio, his so-called brother Alfredo and Harry Stapley. Then she told all she knew about Toddy and explained her fears for Foxy Fanfare. When she had finished she said, "Can you believe all or any of that?"

"Every word!" said the old lady. "I learned long ago that truth is stranger than fiction and the world is full of rogues." She laughed at Ann's startled expression but made no effort to enlighten her further on that point.

"So to recap," she said briskly. "Tell me if I have understood it correctly." She began to tick off the various points on her fingers.

"Firstly, some men made a bomb and we think they hid it in the dressing-up box and then later moved it."

Ann nodded and Madame Pavlova continued.

"We think Julio and Alfredo are posing as Italians but are in fact from somewhere else. They have been heard speaking in a different language and Alfredo did not understand Italian."

"That's right."

"Well, we can soon put that to the test," said the old lady. "I speak Italian with a passable accent – we spent a succession of summers on Lake Como when I was a girl. My parents had a villa there. I had an Italian tutor. I loathed him but he did manage to teach me some Italian." She laughed and moved on to the next point. "Harry Stapley isn't what he seems to be – at least we suspect him of being involved. And, very important, what has happened to the *real* entertainments manager? He might be in trouble, too."

Ann nodded. "I'd forgotten about Bob Stuart," she confessed.

"We also have strong grounds for suspecting that Toddy does not have Foxy Fanfare's interests at heart but might be using them in some way for his own ends."

"He is a compulsive gambler," added Ann.

"Good point! So he might be in financial difficulties and desperate."

Madame Pavlova leaned back. "Is Toddy in league with Stapley and the Ferenzos? And what do any of them hope to gain by blowing up the ship?"

Ann watched her anxiously. Her earlier opinion of the old lady had been modified by her quick grasp of the facts and by her acceptance that Ann was not putting two and two together to make five.

Madame Pavlova was deep in thought and her long fingers drummed impatiently on the bedcover. Ann said nothing, afraid to interrupt her train of thought.

At last Madame Pavlova smiled. "Perhaps I should take a look at the contents of Julio's wallet," she suggested calmly. "I could easily get hold of it. Alfredo's, too."

"But how?" said Ann.

"Remember the watch and the bow tie?"

For a few seconds Ann stared at her blankly but then she laughed aloud. Of course. The sleight of hand with Jay as a victim!

"I shall go right away," said the old lady, rising to her feet and smoothing the creases from her pink dress as calmly as though she had been suggesting a stroll on the deck.

"Do you need any help?" asked Ann. "Someone to distract their attention?"

"No dear, thank you. I have had lots of practice!" There was a gleam in her eye.

She moved towards the door. "But you can see how it's done, if you're interested."

Ann jumped to her feet. "Yes, please!"

"They won't even know they've been robbed," said Madame Pavlova, "because as soon as we've had a look at the contents of the wallets I'll put them back."

Ann smothered a desire to giggle. The situation had been confused before but now it was crazy!

Madame Pavlova gave her a conspiratorial wink and said, "Let's go then."

And Ann could only nod her head.

Eight

Following Madame Pavlova at a discreet distance as instructed, Ann found herself on the boat deck. Ahead of them Julio and Alfredo were leaning on the ship's rail, their heads close together in earnest conversation.

Ann watched, fascinated, as the old lady wandered along towards them on tottery legs, her hair blown by the sea breeze, her skirt fluttering round her thin legs.

At her approach Julio gave her a quick glance but then ignored her. Ann held her breath.

Just as the old lady reached them she stumbled and for a moment Ann was fooled. She saw the old lady pitch forward and clutch at Julio's sleeve to save herself. Somehow she pulled him off balance so that he, too, fell to the deck. Then Alfredo was bending over them, helping the old lady while Julio scrambled to his feet unaided, his face red with annoyance as he brushed down his trousers.

Several other passengers who had seen the incident rushed to offer assistance and Ann saw Madame Pavlova being helped to a deck chair while someone picked up her handbag and someone else hurried away to fetch her a cup of tea.

Reluctantly, Ann tore herself away and returned to her cabin, anxiety mingling with amusement. Ten minutes later there was another tap at her door and Madame Pavlova came in, smiling broadly.

From her handbag she produced two wallets and together they went through the contents.

"We must keep everything in order," warned the old lady, "so that they don't suspect. Now let's see – driving licence in the name of – damnation!" she tutted. "Alfredo Ferenzo. Address in Sorrento. They're cleverer than we thought!"

Ann was looking through the other wallet. "Lots of money but is it Italian?" she asked.

Madame Pavlova glanced at it.

"That's not lire," she said. "I don't recognize it but I'd guess at Arabic. Now what else have we got here? A few photographs of Alfredo himself but taken where?" She frowned with concentration. "Could be the Mediterranean – there's a whitewashed building in the background. It's hard to say. Here's another – taken coming down the steps of an aeroplane but I can't see a thing to tell which airline it is."

Ann said, "Nothing much here – except some English banknotes – thirty five pounds' worth; a business card in the name of Julio Ferenzo for a firm of consultants in New York—"

"So some connection with the U.S.A.," muttered the old lady. "And here we have a couple of receipts from W.H. Smith's bookshop so that proves he can read, if nothing else!"

Ann laughed which helped to release some of the tension building within her. Handling somebody else's wallet made her feel very guilty and although she knew it was in a good cause that fact did not make it any easier.

The result of their search was disappointing. As they returned everything to its proper place Ann said, "So, what have we learned, if anything?"

Madame Pavlova pursed her lips. "Not as much as I'd hoped but we do know they are not amateurs. The false papers are very good and we can assume they've got passports in the name of Ferenzo. I'd guess they're part of a bigger group and not working alone. That makes them much more dangerous."

"The trouble is," said Ann, "that we still have no way of proving the truth of our suspicions. The captain won't want to believe any of it and you can't blame him. The contents of the wallets don't help and—"

Madame Pavlova rose to her feet. "Talking of wallets," she said. "I must return these to their rightful owners before they find out that they're gone."

"But how?" asked Ann. "They'll never believe it if you fall over again!"

"Fall over? Good heavens no!" she said. "Once was enough. No, I shall be thanking them for their help and clutching at them and generally fussing round them the way silly old ladies do. Don't you worry. I shall stage-manage it perfectly." She laughed and left Ann smiling.

While she was away Ann wrestled with the problem of proof but could not think of any way of convincing the captain, unless they could persuade him that Alfredo and his brother were using false papers. If the captain knew that they were pretending to be Italian but did not understand the language he must surely find that suspicious.

She waited impatiently for Madame Pavlova to return but time passed and there was no sign of her. Presumably she was having a job finding them.

The more Ann thought about the brothers and the language, the more she thought she had found the answer. But if the captain let them know that they were under suspicion they might decide not to use the bomb; they might be scared off.

"But would that be a good thing?" she asked aloud.

Or would it mean that they would merely delay their plan until another voyage where they could carry out the plan undetected.

"Ideally we ought to catch them red-handed," she reasoned and then glanced at her watch. Where on earth was Madame Pavlova? Ten minutes later she had still not returned and when footsteps sounded outside Ann jumped thankfully to her feet. However, it was Jay who burst in, his face flushed with anger. He slammed the door behind him and hurled himself onto the bed.

"It's not fair!" he cried.

"Jay!" said Ann. "What's not fair?"

By way of answer, Jay kicked wildly with his legs and then, turning over, began to pound the pillow with his clenched fists.

"I hate everyone!" he shouted. "Everyone is a hateful pig! Everyone!"

She took hold of him and shook him fiercely.

"Tell me what's happened!" she insisted.

To her surprise he suddenly went limp and began to cry.

"Oh Jay, don't!" She said. She knelt on the bed beside him and put her arms round him.

"I hate him," he sobbed. "I do. I hate, hate, HATE him! I'll never sail on this beastly ship again. Never! Never! I shall tell Dad and he'll have to let me fly."

Gradually Ann managed to calm him down until he had recovered sufficiently to accept a bundle of paper tissues on which to blow his nose. Finally he sighed deeply and gazed at Ann, his expression forlorn and his cheeks blotched with the effort of so many tears.

Ann gave him a hug. "Now tell me," she coaxed. "Who is it you hate?"

"The captain," muttered Jay.

"But why? What's he done?"

"He's a mean, rotten pig! That's why."

"But what has he done that's mean and rotten?"

"He's put me out of bounds!" said Jay. "I can't go anywhere on the ship except this cabin, the dining room and the games room." Fresh tears welled up in his eyes. "I can't even go to the lido! It's not fair!"

Ann took a deep breath and counted to ten.

"You mean he's put parts of the ship out of bounds to you," she said. "Well, that's tough, I agree, but why did he do it, Jay? He must have had a good reason."

Jay's expression was now sullen.

"Because of that man with Foxy Fanfare," he said. "It's all his stupid fault."

"You mean Mr Todd, their manager? But how is it his fault?"

"Because he went running to the captain, moaning about me!" cried Jay, his tone aggrieved. "He said I was shadowing him but I wasn't. I just *happened* to be walking in the same direction. But a little way behind him. That's all."

"Jay!" Ann sat on her own bed and regarded him severely.

"Well, I may have been *sort* of following him but I had to. He looked as though he was up to something. You know what I mean."

"Guilty, do you mean?"

Jay nodded. "He kept looking over his shoulder to see if anyone was following him and he went through a door marked CREW ONLY. He

65

shouldn't have been down there but I thought if he can go there then why can't I? So I followed him. He went down some ladders into a great big room and he had his swimming things rolled up under his arm. I was keeping well back – I do *know* how to shadow people—"

"Go on," said Ann.

"It looked like an engine room and it was very noisy and suddenly I caught my foot and fell and he heard me. He came rushing back and grabbed me by my collar and kept shaking me and jabbering something. He was all red in the face and furious. He was *spitting*. Ugh!"

Ann's heart was thumping. Perhaps she had been wrong to keep Jay unaware of what was going on. It sounded as though he had blundered into near disaster.

"I kicked and struggled and then I bit his hand and he let go and started sucking his hand. He tried to catch me but I ran and ran and I got away." He waited hopefully for Ann to congratulate him on his escape but she just nodded. He went on resignedly. "The next thing was that I had to go to the captain and he put me out of bounds. Pig-face was there – I mean Mr Todd – and he said I'd been annoying him and calling him names and I was a pest and – kids like me shouldn't be allowed on ships with decent people." He gulped miserably.

"Did you tell the captain he'd been down to the engine room?"

"Yes, but Pig-face said he hadn't and that I was a liar and he'd been on his way to the lido for a swim. He still had his rolled up towel so the captain believed him."

Ann sat back helplessly. It was as she had suspected – if the captain would not believe Jay then he certainly would not believe anything so far-fetched as a bomb.

Wearily she said, "And is that all, Jay? There's nothing you haven't told me?"

He thought hard. "Only about the man whose wallet had been stolen."

Ann sat bolt upright, pale with shock. "Which man?" she demanded. "Describe him to me quickly!"

To her horror Jay's description fitted Julio to perfection. So Julio *had* missed the wallet. What had happened, then, when Madame Pavlova tried to replace it? Had she been detected? Worse still, had she been arrested as a thief?

Trying to keep her voice steady she asked, "Did the man know who had stolen it?"

"No. At least he didn't say so."

Ann put a hand to her head. Had Julio reported it missing before Madame Pavlova tried to return it? If only she could think straight.

"Well, Jay," she said. "Don't feel too badly about everything. *I* believe you about Pig-face even if the captain doesn't. I think he *is* a crook but I can't prove it yet. He could be dangerous, Jay, so I think you'd better stick to the games room from now on unless we're together. Then I think it won't matter. Give your face a wash with cold water and then when you feel better go and play Space Invaders."

"Then you're not mad at me?"

She looked at him and grinned. "No, I'm not mad," she told him.

"I'm just glad you're safe!" she thought and made her way back to the main deck.

Nine

Just outside the library she met Marion who was pinning a notice on the board. She smiled when she saw Ann.

"Good news," she said. "Foxy Fanfare will be able to play tonight after all."

"Was there some doubt then?" asked Ann.

"Well, their manager was a bit worried about them first thing this morning," Marion confided. "It seemed they were utterly exhausted and he couldn't wake them. He said they sometimes take sleeping pills and he thought they'd taken too many. I've just seen him, though, and they're fine now. Don't want to disappoint the passengers if we can help it."

Suddenly Ann's spirits lifted a little. The prospect of seeing Sam, Mick and Foxy more than made up for the traumas of the past few hours.

Marion said, "I heard all about Jay's performance last night. Seems he now wants to be a conjuror!"

They both laughed but the reference to Madame Pavlova jogged Ann's memory.

"I'm looking for Madame Pavlova," she said casually. "I don't suppose you've seen her anywhere have you?"

Marion's face clouded over and Ann's heart skip-ped a beat.

"Haven't you heard?" asked Marion. "The poor old thing's had some kind of seizure."

"A – a seizure?" cried Ann. "But that's impos-sible! I mean, I was talking to her less than an hour ago. She was in perfect health then." White-faced and shaken she gazed at Marion. "A seizure? I just don't believe it!"

Marion was shaking her head sympathetically. "It was very sudden," she agreed, "but of course she's not young. You know how these old troopers are. Sometimes they go on long after they should. It's as though they can't resist the lime-light, or the smell of the greasepaint. I heard of a chap once, a comedian, who actually died on stage!"

"Where did it happen?" asked Ann, almost fear-fully.

"She was with Mr Stapley," said Marion. "They were leaning over the dressing-up box – looking for something I suppose. Poor Mr Stapley. It gave him a terrible shock. One minute she was fine, the next minute she gave a sort of moan and fell forward." She looked at Ann anxiously. "Are you OK?" she asked. "You look as though you've seen a ghost."

"I want to see her," said Ann. "I must see her."

Marion looked surprised at her vehemence. "I suppose you could ask the doctor," she said doubt-fully. "Madame Pavlova's in the ship's hospital. I doubt if she's well enough to see visitors but you could ask."

Ann thanked her and began to walk towards the lift. Was it possible that the excitement had affected the old lady's health? Just possible – but very unlikely. It was also possible that she had been spotted replacing the stolen wallet and that the bombers had retaliated. Surely it was significant that she had been with Harry Stapley when she was taken ill. And whatever could she have been looking for in the dressing-up box?

She could hardly wait to see Sam, there was so much she had to tell him.

The ship's hospital was in a quiet part of the ship, away from most of the busy passenger areas. Ann had been there on previous occasions and found it again with no trouble. Mrs Atkinson, the middle-aged nurse, looked up as she went in and Ann smiled, hoping her nervousness did not show.

"It's about Madame Pavlova," she said. "I heard that she had been taken ill. How is she?"

"As well as can be expected," said the nurse. Her tone was flat and professional. "She's had a very nasty turn, poor soul, and she's over seventy. At that age it's hard to say what her chances are. So many factors come into it."

Ann's face drained of colour. Was the nurse trying to suggest that Madame Pavlova might *die*? It was impossible. The old lady's words rang in her ears. "I'm one of the world's survivors."

"But surely her chances are good?" she stammered. "She was with me shortly before it happened and she was perfectly OK. Lively as a cricket. She *can't* die!"

The nurse said quickly, "Oh dear no! We certainly hope not. Who said anything about dying?"

"But you aren't sure?"

"People of her age are sometimes affected by shock as much as anything. We have no medical background to refer to. Her own doctor would have a better chance of diagnosing the exact nature of her—"

Ann gasped. "You mean you don't know what's wrong with her?"

The nurse seemed offended by this apparent slur on the doctor and drew herself up stiffly. "Miss Burnside, we are doing all we can for her. I can assure you Madame Pavlova is getting the best possible treatment."

"But how can you treat her if you don't know what's wrong with her?"

"We can stabilize her condition," said the nurse coldly, "and that is what we are doing. When we have something more definite to go on we will—"

"I'd like to see the doctor."

"I'm afraid that won't be possible," the nurse told her. "Only relatives may visit a seriously ill patient."

"But she has no relatives – I'm a friend."

"Friends are not allowed—"

But at that moment the doctor himself appeared, his face anxious.

"Ah Miss Burnside—" he began but the nurse interrupted him.

"I was just telling Miss Burnside that we are doing all we can for Madame Pavlova," she said.

The doctor nodded but turned towards Ann. "You'd better come with me," he said. "Madame Pavlova is barely conscious and she keeps asking to see you."

Ann stepped forward eagerly but the doctor held up a hand to delay her.

"I must explain that she is very weak," he told Ann. "I want to sedate her but I am afraid that if I do I won't be able to monitor her progress as accurately as I can if she is conscious. It's really quite baffling. I have to admit her symptoms puzzle me."

The nurse busied herself with some papers with an air of disapproval but Ann had eyes only for the doctor.

He went on, "It's not a stroke and it's not a heart attack. It's not epilepsy, or apoplexy. She seems to be losing body heat—"

Ann said, "Body heat? I don't think I understand."

"Her temperature is dropping rapidly—" He broke off and shook his head. "Anyway, she is very insistent that she sees you. Perhaps she will be a little easier in her mind after your visit."

He led the way into the hospital and Ann followed him. The hospital consisted of a large airy ward containing six beds. There was a desk at one end and a young nurse, busy on the telephone, looked up as they entered.

"Any luck?" The doctor asked but she shook her head.

"We're trying to trace her GP," the doctor told Ann. "Her family doctor, that is. If she had one. Some people with good health never need a doctor."

Madame Pavlova lay in bed, her head supported by a pile of pillows. She wore a white hospital gown, her fluffy hair was pinned back and all her gaudy make-up had been removed. She looked years older. An electrocardiograph stood on a table beside her bed. Across the screen a small white blip traced a regular pattern of dips and curves.

A young member of the crew lay in the opposite bed reading a copy of the Readers Digest and he smiled at Ann. "Poor old girl," he said, with a jerk of his head at the inert form in the opposite bed. "She's in a bad way. Hope she doesn't croak on me."

Ann swallowed hard. Madame Pavlova lay so still that for a terrible moment Ann thought she was already dead. Her face was ashen, the skin drawn tightly over the cheekbones. Long fingers clutched the bedclothes and her knuckles were white. But it was the eyes that frightened Ann most. The blue eyes which so recently had been full of understanding and humour were now almost black. She seemed to stare fixedly at nothing and her lips were blue-grey.

Ann leaned over her and said, "It's me, Madame Pavlova. It's Ann Burnside. Can you hear me? Can you understand?"

At first there was no response but then, with painful slowness, the old lady moved her head.

Ann glanced helplessly at the doctor but he merely shrugged his shoulders.

"Do you want to tell me something?" Ann persisted.

Was it her imagination or did the bony fingers tighten on the bedcover. The blue lips parted. "Need," she whispered. "Need."

"You need something?" asked Ann. "Tell me what you need." A muscle twitched in the old lady's cheek and her fingers moved again.

"Need—" she repeated.

The doctor said, "That's all I could get out of her. That and something that sounded like 'Poy', or 'Boy'. Oh, and your name, of course."

Madame Pavlova began to cough suddenly and the doctor tried to persuade her to take a sip of water.

"We may have to put her on a drip," he muttered, more to himself than Ann.

He laid her back against the pillows and Ann leaned over her again. "Can you tell me what happened?" she asked.

The voice was so weak. "Need—" Suddenly her head slumped forward on her chest.

Ann looked at her fearfully.

75

The doctor glanced at the screen beside her and took hold of the old lady's wrist.

His frown deepened. "She's very weak," he told Ann. "And getting weaker by the minute! If only I could establish what it is. I've done a few tests and have sent them by satellite to New York for analysis."

"Will the results come in time?"

"I certainly hope so." He shook his head. "I keep wondering if she's been abroad recently and maybe picked up one of those obscure tropical diseases. I've seen most diseases but this one has me baffled."

Ann stayed at the old lady's bedside for another ten minutes but Madame Pavlova did not regain consciousness and at last the doctor persuaded her to go.

"There's nothing you can do," he told her gently. "I'll let you know at once if there's any change in her condition."

Ann moved towards the door in a state of deep depression. All thoughts of the bombers had fled from her mind and all she could think about was the fact that a brave, cheerful old lady might die. She recalled the wink the old lady had given her and heard again her tinkling laugh. Ann's eyes filled with tears and she put up a hand to brush them away. The man in the opposite bed said, "Hey! Cheer up! Come and talk to me for a while. My name's Frank Whitby and I've been stuck here since yesterday without any visitors. It gets lonely in this dump, I can tell you."

Obediently Ann stood by his bed while he told her how he had tipped a pan of boiling water over his leg.

"Only been on the ship an hour," he told her. "Only been in the galley ten minutes – I'm an assistant chef, see – and I go and scald myself. Did I yell!" he grinned.

"I'm so sorry," said Ann mechanically.

"I thought, Oh well, I'll have a cushy trip, lying in the hospital eating grapes but I'm browned off. Sick of my own company."

"Haven't you got any friends?" she asked. "Don't your mates visit you?"

"Not really. This is my first voyage on this ship. Mate of mine got me the job. He's worked on the *Santa Lucia* for years. So I turn up and he didn't! Trust Bob, I thought! We were supposed to make the trip together and then we were going to spend a few hours in Southampton seeing the sights."

Suddenly Ann's tired mind registered what he had said.

"Bob who?" she cried. "The mate who didn't show up!"

"Why, Bob Stuart, but what's it to you?" He looked at her in surprise. "D'you know him then?"

"No, I don't," said Ann. "At least I've seen him before. I've made crossings lots of times. What happened to him? Do you know?"

"He was the entertainments manager."

"Yes, I know. Why didn't he turn up?"

He shook his head. "It was one of those strange things," he said. "We were talking on the phone – making last minute arrangements, so to speak, and suddenly the line went dead. Hello, I thought, they've cut him off. He's forgotten to pay the phone bill!" He laughed and Ann smiled obligingly although her thoughts were racing.

"So when exactly was the phone call?" she asked.

"The night before we were due to sail. I tried to ring him again but no luck so I thought I'd be sure to meet up with him when I got on board." He shrugged. "When I turned up he wasn't here. Just a message to say he was unavoidably detained. Very odd, that, I still can't make it out. He was never ill and he wasn't married so it couldn't have been a family crisis."

"I wonder why his phone went dead?" Ann said slowly. "Could someone have cut the wire?"

His astonishment was obvious. "Cut the telephone wire? Why on earth should anyone do that?"

"A burglar?" said Ann. "A mugger?"

"Oh come off it!" he said scornfully. "Bob didn't have anything worth pinching and he didn't have any enemies." His eyes narrowed suddenly. "Mind you, there was something funny one night I remember. I wasn't there but Bob told me. A man came up to him in a pub and offered him five hundred quid to skip the voyage."

Ann felt her legs go weak. She groped for a chair and sat down suddenly. "Go on!" she told him.

78

"Seems he wanted to get to England to see his girlfriend and said he couldn't afford the fare. Pull the other leg, Bob told him. It's got bells on!" He laughed. "If he could give Bob five hundred quid then he could afford the fare, couldn't he? Not a very good liar, was he? Bob wouldn't have anything to do with it. Said it might lose him his job but this bloke was determined. Offered him a cool thousand!"

Ann gasped.

"I'd have been sorely tempted," Frank admitted, "but not Bob. Straight as a die, Bob is."

"And you don't know this man's name or what he looked like?"

He shrugged. "Search me!"

Ann stood up and his face fell.

"Oh, you're not going already?"

"I have to," she told him. "But if you like I'll send you some grapes! Which do you prefer – black or white?"

"You mean it?"

"Brownie's honour!"

"White then – and better make them seedless! Can't go spitting grape seeds all over the place. Nursie won't like it." He raised his voice for the benefit of the nurse but she was still talking on the telephone and took no notice.

Before leaving the ward Ann went back for a last look at Madame Pavlova but the old lady looked so near to death that she could not bear it.

With a final word for Frank she made her

way out of the hospital and back to her cabin.

As she opened the door she saw that an envelope had been pushed under it in her absence. She opened it with trembling fingers, fearing more bad news but as she read it she let out a shriek of joy. It was from Sam and within minutes she was running along the passage on her way to meet him.

Ten

Although the breeze was quite fresh, they stood together at the rail because Ann wanted to be sure that what she had to tell Sam would not be overheard.

"I was so sure that something dreadful had happened to you," she told him. "I began to think you were never going to reappear and I was so pleased when Marion said you *would* be performing tonight. What kept you?"

He seemed amused by her question.

"Nothing particular," he told her. "I suppose we were so exhausted that we slept right round the clock. Foxy and Mick are still asleep."

"And that's all?"— Ann persisted. "You don't think Toddy drugged you?"

"Drugged us? Why should he?"

"To keep you away from people. I don't know really."

Even as she said it she knew how feeble it sounded.

Sam looked at he soberly. "Look Ann," he said. "I know Foxy said some nasty things about him and that's made you suspicious but I honestly don't think

81

he's a crook or anything. He gambles and loses money and we don't much like him but he's not a crook. At least, I don't think he is."

"What do you know about his background?" Ann asked. "I mean, is he married, single. Does he have any children?"

"He was married once, a long time ago, but it didn't last. His wife left him and took their little boy. His father's still alive but lives in America; his mother died so I suppose you could say he has no one."

"Except his son."

"I guess so."

"Does he talk about him?"

"Not much, but he has a few photographs. He's an odd character and not very likeable but I feel a bit sorry for him. I don't think he'd hurt anyone."

"He didn't give you any tablets last night?"

"No. Just the usual vitamin stuff. It's pretty awful but we take it just to please him. He's a bit of a health freak on the quiet! Always has been. It's just carrot juice and egg and fruit and stuff, all whipped up in a blender. It's a sort of pick-me-up. Gives you energy. He swears by it and it's never done us any harm."

"Did it taste exactly the same as usual?"

He considered the question carefully, his head on one side.

"I guess not," he said at last, "but then he doesn't always use the same ingredients. Sometimes he puts cranberry juice in it – that's rather good. Sometimes it's bananas but that makes it rather thick and squelchy."

"So you don't think you were made to sleep that long?"

"No, I don't think so."

Ann was silent for a while, trying to assess what he had told her in the light of the rest of her evidence. While she was thinking Sam remained quiet and Ann, glancing at him, thought how calm he was; how very different from his excitable sister. His auburn hair glinted in the sunlight and his freckles were more pronounced. When she still did not speak he turned his grey eyes on her and said, "Hadn't you better tell me what all this is about? I can see there's something worrying you."

"I will," said Ann, "but it will take a long time and if, when I've told you, you don't believe me, I shall –" she glanced round in mock desperation, "I shall throw myself into the sea!"

"I'll believe you," he promised. "Hand on heart!"

Haltingly, she began her story and the telling of it was not easy. There were so many separate strands and so many loose ends. Even to her own ears it sounded highly unlikely. How on earth, she wondered, was anyone else going to believe it?"

When she had finished she waited for Sam's verdict with crossed fingers. If he did not believe her she was lost.

The silence lengthened and then he said, "What

was that word that Madame Pavlova kept saying."

So he did believe her, she thought, and relief filled her.

"Need?"

"Not that one. The one the doctor mentioned."

"It was either poy or boy but that doesn't make much sense."

"Suppose it was only part of a word," he suggested, trying not to let his excitement show. "Suppose it was *poi*son and suppose need was only half a word. That could have been *need*le."

Ann was so startled she could only stare at him in shocked admiration.

"You mean someone –" She shook her head. "But how could anyone do that without her knowing? It would be impossible to give someone an injection without someone else seeing what was happening."

He screwed up his face with the effort of concentration. "It could be done," he said. "I remember reading in the paper some years ago about a spy who was poisoned with the spike of an umbrella. There was a needle concealed in the umbrella point and someone pretended to bump into the spy and jabbed him with the umbrella spike."

"I remember that too," she said.

"Has the doctor considered poisons?" asked Sam. Ann shook her head.

Sam was thinking it through. "You say she collapsed over that chest. Let's suppose that someone fixed a needle to the inside of the dressing-up box, tricked Madame Pavlova into reaching into the box and then pushed her arm against the needle. If the poison acted quickly enough she'd collapse before she had a chance to tell anybody what had happened."

"And that's what she was trying to tell us! Needle and poison! Oh Sam! I feel sure you're right. But will the doctor believe us?"

"Probably not, but we needn't waste time trying to explain our suspicions. It would probably be enough to suggest that it might be a poison and not a disease. At least he can do the necessary tests then. From what you say I should think he'd be glad to try anything. If we don't say we think someone else has poisoned her he might assume she poisoned herself. Either accidentally or on purpose. It won't matter much what he thinks as long as he can find out which poison it is and give her the correct antidote."

After a brief discussion it was decided that Ann should go alone to the hospital and she set off at once. The doctor listened to her idea with obvious surprise but he did not rule it out immediately as she had feared he might. "I'll certainly do some tests right away," he told Ann, "but I have to admit that I don't see how a poison could have been introduced into her body. She obviously has no enemies, and why should she want to kill herself?"

"I don't know," said Ann, not meeting his gaze.

"Anything is worth a try," he said. "I'll go and

look at her now in the light of what you have suggested, but please don't raise your hopes too high. She is very elderly and her conditions is—"

At that moment the young nurse who Ann had seen earlier ran towards them looking very agitated.

"Please come quickly doctor!" she cried. "It's Madame Pavlova. Her pulse is almost gone!"

Ann's own heart was beating very rapidly as she followed the doctor along the corridor and into the ward. The blip on the screen beside Madame Pavlova was behaving very erratically – varying from a huge loop to almost none at all – and Ann found the electronic sound sinister.

The doctor was beside the old lady in seconds and snapping out orders to the nurse who moved quickly and efficiently to obey them.

Frank called Ann over. "Be all over in a minute," he forecast gloomily. "Poor old thing! I could see it coming."

In a choked voice Ann said, "She wasn't a poor old thing at all. She was shrewd, wise and very kind. She mustn't die, mustn't . . ." Unable to bear the sight of the doctor's ministrations, she sat down beside Frank and closed her eyes. "Please God, don't let her die," she prayed. "Please let the doctor save her."

She heard the doctor say, "Quickly! Quickly!" but the hateful blip continued to slow down.

Frank said, "We've all got to go sometime, you know. She's had a good long life."

Ann nodded without answering.

The nurse's footsteps sounded on the linoleum as she ran along the ward and then the doors were flung open as she rushed out. Still Ann dared not look round. More footsteps as the nurse returned and then the doctor muttered his thanks for whatever it was that she had been sent to fetch.

Suddenly she heard the doctor say, "Good! Well done nurse!"

Ann glanced toward the bed and met the doctor's eye.

"I think we've caught her in time," he said. "I think she's safe for the moment."

Ann breathed a sigh of relief and went towards Madame Pavlova's bed. The doctor was shining a light into the old lady's eyes.

"You may be right," he told Ann. "It could be a poison. Amazing." He shook his head. "The things I learn in this job."

He sent the nurse scurrying away for various items which he would need for the tests and took the old lady's thin wrist between his fingers. "Much stronger," he said approvingly.

On the screen Ann saw that the blip was once more maintaining a regular pattern and, glancing upwards, she whispered, "Thank you!"

The doctor smiled at her. "You can stop worrying for a while," he said. "We've averted that particular disaster. Her condition is stable, as we say."

Ann thanked him and took the hint, giving Frank a cheerful wave as she left the ward. She went straight to the shop that sold flowers and fruit and ordered a bunch of crysanthemums for Madame Pavlova. When she recovered consciousness she would see them. For Frank she ordered white seedless grapes and asked for them to be delivered to the ward.

Then she went in search of Sam and found him in the pool with Foxy. Mick and Toddy, apparently were playing deck quoits elsewhere. With Ann's permission, Sam told Foxy all that Ann had told him and she listened with rapt attention.

Teatime came and they sat together eating cream puffs and trying to decide on a plan of action. Ann thought they might question the crew about Bob Stuart but it did seem improbable that anyone would know more than Frank about what had happened.

"If only the police could search his flat they might find him tied up," Foxy suggested. "Unless, of course, he's been kidnapped. It might be a much bigger gang than we think. Someone on shore might be getting messages to the bombers."

"How could they do it?" asked Ann.

They all pondered the problem.

"They could send a radio message in code," said Sam. "Not the type that has to be decoded but the sort that says, 'My aunt has now arrived' – meaning a person or a shipment of gold or something. They do it all the time on the television."

"I wish this was a TV plot instead of real life," said Ann wistfully. "I was so looking forward to the trip."

Foxy nodded. "It's put me right off being a private detective," she admitted. "Much too scary."

Suddenly Foxy clapped her hands. "I've got it!" she cried, "and don't bother to tell me I'm a genius because I know it! We send an anonymous letter to the captain telling him to check up on Bob Stuart! He may not really believe it but he might act on it."

"Why should he?" Sam objected. "He'll probably think it's a hoax."

"Ah, but will he dare risk ignoring it?" Foxy demanded. "After all, it would look bad if he ignored the message and there was some truth in it. He might follow it up just to be on the safe side."

It did seem a possibility and after further discussion, they still could not think of anything else to do.

"Who's going to write it?" asked Sam. "I will if you like. I'll use capital letters so that—"

"Why should you do it?" Foxy demanded. "It's Ann who's got the information."

He shrugged. "I'm older than the rest of you, that's all."

"So what?" Foxy tossed her head. "What you really mean is that a mere slip of a girl like Ann—"

Ann held up a hand for peace. "I don't think any of us should write it," she said. "They might recognize the handwriting. If it's supposed to be anonymous we should cut words out of a newspaper."

Sam said, "That's a brilliant idea."

She smiled at him. "And thanks for the offer,"

she said. "I know you meant it for the right reasons."

They could not include Nick since he was with Toddy but they armed themselves with scissors and glue and went down to Ann's cabin.

After much argument they decided the message should read: "WHAT HAS HAPPENED TO BOB STUART STOP ALERT THE POLICE"

It was surprisingly slow work finding suitable words or parts of words to make up the message but at last they assembled them all and pasted them onto a sheet of the ship's notepaper.

"How do we get it to him?" Ann asked. "We can hardly ask one of the crew to deliver it."

They talked it over and it was finally decided that one of them would drop it near to the captain's chair during dinner. Someone would find it and give it to him.

The captain would be dining in the first class restaurant and Ann and Jay would be in the other one. It would have to be a job for Foxy Fanfare. Sam volunteered but Foxy insisted that she should do it as it was originally her idea. Wisely Sam did not suggest that it was too risky for a girl to undertake. He would have been howled down!

"Oh dear!" said Ann. "I shan't be able to enjoy my dinner because I'll be wondering what's happening."

"Don't let it spoil your appetite," laughed Foxy. "We'll tell you all about it."

That evening Ann and Jay went into dinner and

sat down at the table for six which had been allotted to them. They shared it with two middle-aged sisters and a couple called Day. They were greeted by their two favourite stewards, Tony and Simon.

Jay studied the menu and then looked up at Simon who waited to take the order.

"Let me guess," said Simon. "Sausages and chips?"

It was Jay's staple diet.

Jay, used to his teasing, said, "Not today, thank you. I'll have chips and sausages instead!"

Tony handed round the basket of bread rolls and said, "It looks as if no one wants to sit with you tonight."

Ann glanced at the four empty chairs and laughed.

"The two sisters are probably still in the theatre," she told him. "They're showing Lawrence of Arabia again and they said they were going to see it. I expect they'll be along later. I don't know about Mr and Mrs Day."

Jay said, "I should think they're still full from the whopping lunch they ate!"

"Jay!" giggled Ann, but she let the remark pass.

She ordered smoked salmon salad and ice cream but she ate it distractedly, her mind on what was happening in the other restaurant.

They were joined half way through the meal by the two sisters who told them all about the film at great length. Ann listened as politely as she could but as soon as the meal was over she hurried to meet up with Sam and Foxy and learn what had happened.

"Worked like a dream!" Foxy enthused. "Nobody saw me drop it and a few minutes later one of the stewards noticed it and handed it to the captain."

Sam took up the story. "He looked rather puzzled and then half turned away from the other people on the table and opened it up. When he read it he shook his head a couple of times and then excused himself from the table."

"He went to another table," said Foxy, "and showed it to one of his officers – the one with very blond hair."

"Mr Cox," said Ann, who knew their names.

"He got up as well and they both went out of the dining room."

Ann patted Foxy on the back. "Congratulations!" she cried.

Sam said, "We don't know whether or not they contacted the London police but at least they took it seriously. The captain must have been in touch with the company. He would ask his office in New York what to do. They might have passed it on to the police. Perhaps at this very moment a panda car is on its way to rescue Bob Stuart."

"Let's hope he's still alive!" said Foxy and they all stared at her in horror.

"Surely they wouldn't *kill* him!" Ann protested. "They only wanted to take his place on the ship."

Foxy shrugged. "Maybe he put up a fight—"

Ann said quickly, "I don't even want to think about it! Things are bad enough already."

They went for a walk along the deck for half an hour but then Foxy and Sam were due back to prepare for the evening's performance.

Suddenly Sam stopped abruptly in his tracks. "I don't want to worry you," he said, "but—"

"You've worried me!" cried Foxy. "Whatever is it now?"

"It's about that note," said Sam. "I've just realized that the captain's going to guess that it wasn't sent by an adult. You see an adult would know that the captain would take him – or her – seriously. Or at least listen politely. An adult wouldn't need to send a note. That means he'll know it must be a child or a teenager. Not many children would used the word ALERT. That narrows it down quite a bit. I just think we ought to be prepared in case one of us is summoned to the captain's cabin."

Ann sighed. "Then he's sure to suspect me," she told them, "because Jay and I always seem to be in trouble. They'd never accuse you because you're Foxy Fanfare."

"She's right," said Foxy. "So you should plan what to say if—"

There was a shout and they looked round to see Mick beckoning. "Come on, you two!" he shouted to Foxy and Sam. "Toddy's blowing a gasket! He's getting so worked up he'll lay an egg in a minute!"

Foxy grinned. "We're coming! Keep your wig on!"

To Ann she said, "We have to go. See you at the show – that is, if you're coming."

"Try and stop me!" said Ann with a grin.

Eleven

She went in search of Jay who was in the games room to see if he wanted to go to the show.

"I can't," he said plaintively, "because the hateful old pig of a captain—"

"Hush Jay!" Ann said hastily, clapping a hand over his mouth. "I'm sure you can come to the show with me. I think the captain only wants to stop you wandering about alone. He's not too keen on you shadowing people."

With this assurance, Jay allowed himself to be prised away from his video games and they hurried to the main lounge and found two seats near the front.

When the lights dimmed and Harry Stapley appeared Ann was tempted to boo him! The wretched man had tried to kill Madame Pavlova and now he had the gall to stand in front of the audience, apologizing for the fact that she was unable to appear due to ill health!

"Her place will be taken by one of the passengers – Mr Stephen King," he told them, "who is – er, who has agreed at very short notice to entertain us.

Mr King is well known in musical circles and opera lovers will be delighted to –" He stopped abruptly as all heads turned away from him to watch the captain. He was making his way between the seats to stand beside Harry Stapley. In his hand he held a sheet of paper and for a moment Ann's heart stood still. Surely he was not going to read out the note they had sent! She felt herself go hot and then cold as panic flared. He was going to denounce her as a troublemaker!

Had there been a convenient crack in the floor she would have crawled into it!

The captain spoke in a low voice to Harry Stapley and Ann, watching closely, fancied that the entertainments manager turned a little pale. Then the captain moved to the microphone and cleared his throat. The audience fell silent and listened to his words.

"Ladies and gentlemen," he began in a voice that trembled with outrage. "I have just received the following message by radio. I have to say that I do not entirely believe the allegations but after consultation with the company's New York office I have decided to conduct a thorough search of the ship. This will set all our minds at ease."

Already a great muttering ran through the audience as the passengers realized what he was about to say. He held up a hand for silence and began to read:

"There is a bomb on board the *Santa Lucia* Stop

We demand the release of Abd el Rahman Stop You have until midnight to arrange this Stop If not the bomb will be detonated."

He lowered the paper and the muttering became a roar as everyone began talking at once. For a few moments the captain made no move to stop them. He turned and spoke to Harry Stapley again and the latter shook his head.

Ann looked at Jay in dismay.

"I told you there was a bomb," he said smugly. He seemed quite unafraid.

"So we were too late!" she whispered.

"Too late for what?"

"We tried to warn the captain," she told him. "We sent an anonymous letter hinting that something was wrong."

Frantically, she tried to work out whether or not this message told her anything useful. It was now certain there were other members of the gang for who could have sent the letter? What on earth would the captain do about it? And who on earth was Abd el Rahman? Where was he imprisoned, she wondered, and would the authorities release him? If not, there would almost certainly be an explosion aboard the *Santa Lucia*. If it was large enough it might sink them.

She remembered reading about the *Titanic*, another luxury liner, which had hit an iceberg many years ago. That had sunk and thousands of people had perished in the icy waters of the Atlantic.

Someone screamed and was immediately hushed. Quickly the captain raised his hand for attention and the voices finally died away.

"Ladies and gentlemen," he began. "I cannot stress too highly the need for complete calm. A panic will not help anyone and it might help the villains who have perpetrated this crime." There was a murmur of approval. "While the search is in progress it will greatly help the crew if all passengers are out of their cabins so we are going to conduct a boat drill which would have taken place tomorrow morning. When I have finished speaking I would like you all to return to your cabins and wait for the alarm bell to sound. The instructions for the drill are on a leaflet which you will find behind your cabin doors."

A man called out, "Why can't we just go up on deck? It would be quicker, wouldn't it?"

The captain nodded. "It would," he agreed, "but then we wouldn't know where everyone was and we need to account for every single passenger and every crew member. Also, an equal number of passengers have been allotted to each lifeboat. We don't want a hundred people waiting for boat number one and five waiting for boat number seven. It's just possible that members of the gang are on board and if anyone is missing after the roll call has been taken it might – I repeat *might* – point us to the guilty party."

Another discussion flared and again the captain

98

waited for an appropriate lull. Ann marvelled at his calm manner.

"I'm sorry that we have to interrupt your evening's entertainment," he went on, "but you will understand that we must treat this seriously. If it is a hoax there is no harm done. If not – if we find an explosive device – we shall immediately obtain the help of suitable experts to defuse it."

Another voice shouted out, "Suppose it's true but you can't find it!"

"We *shall* find it," the captain insisted. "I repeat, ladies and gentlemen, there is no call for alarm. My crew are trained to deal with any emergency."

A woman stood up. "If we have to take the lifeboats, what then? I mean, have we got enough? When the *Titanic* went down there weren't enough lifeboats!"

"The regulations were changed after that disaster, madam," he told her soothingly. "Now it is law that every ship must be adequately provided with lifeboats. Please have no fear on that score."

Someone else called out but the captain shook his head.

"I understand your feelings perfectly" he said. "Believe me, this is a new and difficult experience for all of us but the worst thing we can do is to help the criminals and we will help them if we give way to hysteria. At present there is no danger, ladies and gentlemen. Please return to your cabins, put on your lifejackets and when the alarm bell sounds follow the arrows on the corridor walls to find your allotted boat station. You will then know exactly what to do if there ever is a need to abandon ship."

Jay turned to Ann, his eyes shining with excitement.

"We're going to abandon ship!" he cried. "Oh boy! What an adventure! I forgive old ugly mug—"

"Jay!" she said sternly. "It's not a laughing matter."

By this time half the seats were empty and Ann and Jay joined the throng of people making their way back to their cabins. There was no panic but the strain showed in the passengers' expressions.

Ann was wondering if now was the time to tell the captain all she knew. Now, surely, he would believe her.

Back in the cabin she tied on her orange lifejacket and decided to wait until the crew had searched the ship. Then she could give the captain all the information she had gathered. Finding the bomb and getting it defused was obviously the number one priority.

She helped Jay to fasten his lifejacket and then the alarm bell sounded.

"Remember," said Ann. "No running and don't use the lifts."

"I know!" Jay grumbled. "We've done dozens of drills."

They joined the rest of the passengers who were now making their way along the corridors and up the stairs. They found their boat station and were soon part of a crowd in the charge of Mr Stanley, one of the ship's most experienced senior officers.

He explained that in the case of an emergency the nearest lifeboat would be theirs and that it would be swung out and over the side. When it was in the correct position passengers would be helped into it. And not before! He repeated the captain's assurance that there would be sufficient places on the boats for all passengers and crew.

"I'd just dive over the side!" cried Jay, putting his hands together and pretending to do just that.

Ann whispered, "Stop showing off! You're already in their bad books," but he was too excited to take any notice.

There were about forty people in their group and it was surprising how quickly they began talking to each other as the danger they all shared drew them close.

Ann glanced at her watch. Twenty five minutes had passed since the captain's announcement. Presumably they had not found the bomb yet.

To Mr Stanley she said, "I suppose they'll look in the engine room."

"They'll look everywhere," he replied. "They'll go through the ship with a fine-toothed comb. Don't you worry."

Ann wondered which boat Foxy Fanfare would

101

be in. If they did have to abandon ship it would have been nice to be with Sam.

The sooner she could talk to the captain the better, she thought anxiously.

After another quarter of an hour the passengers were beginning to get a little restless, even bored. The general opinion was that, after all, it must be a hoax.

Suddenly, however, an announcement was made over the loud speaker system which dispelled that theory.

"Ladies and gentlemen. We have now located a small explosive device."

There was a gasp of horror.

"It is situated in the engine room and we have taken all necessary steps to contain the explosion should it be triggered off. An explosives expert will join the ship shortly but in the meantime there is no danger. On behalf of the crew I would like to thank you all for your patience and co-operation. The drill is now at an end. You may continue with your evening's entertainment. Thank you."

So it was all over!

Ann, weak with relief, gave a little cheer as excited chatter broke out all around them. Only Jay looked disappointed.

They returned to their cabin, removed their lifejackets and stowed them away on top of the wardrobe.

"Are you going back to the concert?" Jay asked.

"No," Ann told him grimly. "We're both going to see the captain. Now is the time to tell him all we know."

Twelve

To Ann's relief the captain was willing to talk to them and they were quickly shown into his cabin.

"Please sit down," he told them and they settled themselves in leather covered armchairs.

Ann started at the beginning, explaining what Jay had seen in their old cabin.

The captain looked at Jay. "Well, Master Burnside, it seems we may have been a little hard on you," he said. "Will you tell me in your own words exactly what you saw."

Jay launched into a somewhat exaggerated account of his exploits, and the captain made a few notes on a jotter.

"Ann thought it was putty," Jay told him, "but I knew it wasn't. I knew they were going to sink the *Santa Lucia*."

Ann said, "It sounded so unlikely."

The captain smiled at her. "I sympathize," he said. "I would have thought so too. Please go on, Miss Burnside, with the rest of the story."

She told him bout Julio and Alfredo and about Madame Pavlova.

The captain nodded. "You were right about the poison," he said. "Just before the terrorists' message arrived I had been speaking to the doctor about her condition. He has identified the poison, and we have the antidote. He was pretty hopeful that he could save her life."

Ann then told him about Toddy and her suspicions but the captain did not share her doubts.

"I simply don't see a connection," he told her.

Ann told him about the gambling and suggested that Toddy might be desperate for money. She then told him about her fears for Bob Stuart and he said, "Ah! The anonymous note! I had a feeling you might be responsible for that. Well, on that point you can rest easy for I *have* alerted Scotland Yard and they are investigating the matter."

Determined not to be overlooked for long, Jay piped up again.

"I *knew* there was a bomb in the engine room – at least, I guessed it was."

The captain said, "You really have been tremendously helpful, Master Burnside, but I still think I was right to put certain parts of the ship out of bounds to you. Not, however, for the bombers' sake but for yours. They are desperate and will stop at nothing. I suspect that they might well have retaliated against you in some way if you had bobbed up again."

Jay looked unconvinced by this argument but the captain turned his attention back to Ann.

"Is there anything you haven't told me?" he asked, glancing down at his notes. "If not, then I thank you most sincerely and I'll get on to the company straight away for advice on how to deal with the terrorists."

"There's just one thing," said Ann. "Who is Abd el Rahman?"

"He's a member of a guerrilla group that operates in South America," he told her. "A very nasty piece of work. He's responsible for several bombings and was caught red-handed trying to blow up a supermarket. He was their leader until his arrest a year or so back. At present he is being held in prison somewhere in South America."

Jay piped up. "Aren't you going to arrest them? Aren't you going to catch the bombers?"

"Oh yes!" said the captain. "We'll arrest them, don't you worry, but we have to proceed one step at a time. Our first priority has to be the safety of our passengers so we cannot make any hasty, ill-advised moves that might jeopardize that. We must also, of course, consider the safety of the ship. We must do nothing to precipitate a disaster." He shook his head wearily. "One thing we have to consider is that there might be more than the one bomb we have already found. Never underestimate your enemy! That's the first rule."

At that moment, there was a knock at the door and Mr Clark, one of the ship's senior officers, came in.

"Sir, there's a ship on its way to us, the *Albara*.

She should rendezvous in twenty minutes. She has a Captain Spence on board – a bomb disposal expert. The ship has its own helicopter and they'll fly him over to us if we can make ready a suitable landing place."

"Good show!" cried the captain with heartfelt relief. "I'm beginning to feel distinctly more cheerful, Mr Clark."

Mr Clark grinned. "So am I, sir."

"So am I!" cried Jay.

But for some reason which she could not explain, Ann didn't join in their enthusiasm. It was all going too well, she thought uneasily. Were the bombers really going to give in with so little fight or did they have alternative plans? The stakes were high and they had already taken tremendous risks. Would it all be over in half an hour? She wanted to believe it but she felt she knew the bombers better than the captain did. She had been aware of them for a long time – had thought about almost nothing else. She had been pitting her wits against theirs for what seemed an age and she knew they would not give in gracefully. They had tried to kill Madame Pavlova so they would surely stop at nothing.

With a start, she became aware that the captain was smiling at her. "Do cheer up, Miss Burnside," he said. "You may rest assured that the worst is over."

"I hope so," she said.

"You have my word on it!" he told her.

But at that very moment, as though timed to disprove his words, there was a tremendous explosion which rocked the ship. On the captain's table a vase of flowers toppled and fell, sending a stream of water across the various papers lying there.

The captain cried, "What the—"

Then the lights flickered and they were plunged into darkness. They heard the sounds of running footsteps; people screamed in terror and doors slammed. They heard members of the crew shouting, "Keep calm, everyone! Don't panic!"

"Why doesn't the emergency lighting come on!" cried the captain.

Ann reached out and caught hold of Jay's sleeve. It would be just like him to take advantage of the darkness, and she did not want him wandering off.

"You stay with me, Jay," she warned. "D'you hear?"

"They've blown us up!" he cried, excitedly. "They've really done it. They've – ouch!"

"Keep quiet!" Ann shook him. "This is not a game, Jay. People might be injured or dead."

He tried to tug himself free but she hung on.

A match flared and they watched the captain light a small lamp and set it on his desk.

"You'd better go back to your cabins," he told them, "but use the stairs. The power will be affected and the lifts are either out of order or unreliable."

Ann nodded. "What will you do now?" she asked.

"We shall have to determine the extent of the

damage and then it may be necessary to sound the alarm."

Ann nodded again and still grasping Jay's arm she led him out of the cabin and into the corridor.

She felt badly shaken and not a little frightened although she would never have admitted it.

The corridor seemed to be full of people all with makeshift lights of one kind or another.

"I've got a torch in my drawer," Jay told her but suddenly the overhead lights came on, although with greatly reduced power.

Ann said, "I wonder if Foxy Fanfare are OK?"

It was tempting to go and see but if the ship was badly damaged and had to be abandoned she and Jay must be in the right place at the right time.

They reached their cabin and Jay flung himself cheerfully onto the bed.

"Isn't this exciting!" he cried.

Ann said severely, "Listen to me, Jay. This is not a game. It is very serious – deadly serious in fact – and you have got to behave yourself. If you don't, I shall tell Dad."

"Sneak!"

"Jay, I mean it! If you play up—"

"I know," he said. "I'm sorry. I won't play up. Honest."

"If anything awful happens to you Dad will blame me," she reminded him. "Now get out your torch and we'll play I-spy or something to pass the time."

Fifteen minutes later the captain broadcast another message to the ship. He informed them that the damage had been slight and was confined to the engine room. Fortunately no damage had been done to the ship's hull.

"The *Santa Lucia* is still totally seaworthy," he went on, "and at the present time there is no need to consider the evacuation of the ship. The *Albara* is only miles away and is closing rapidly. Captain Spence, a bomb disposal expert, is on board and he will be flown to the *Santa Lucia* and with several colleagues will undertake another search of the ship. Military personnel will also join us. I beg you to remain calm. There is no danger. You may leave your cabins if you wish but please do nothing to obstruct my officers or Captain Spence's team from carrying out their duties."

Jay jumped to his feet. "Can I go, then?" he asked.

"Yes," she said, after a moment's hesitation. "But remember what I said."

He nodded and the next moment he had gone, leaving Ann to wonder whether she had done the right thing in letting him go.

With a shrug, she decided that it was too late now and turned her thoughts to Sam, Foxy and Mick. And what on earth was Toddy up to?

She would go along and find out.

When she reached Foxy's cabin she knocked at the door but there was no answer. The room steward came out and pointed out the boys' cabin.

110

"But they're not in there," she told Ann. "I knocked a few moments ago. I haven't seen them since before the boat drill."

"What about Mr Todd?" she asked. "Have you seen him?"

The steward shook her head. "I haven't seen any of them," she said. "I expect they've gone somewhere to rehearse for their performance."

Thoughtfully, Ann made her way back to the lift and went up onto the boat deck. Here, in the deepening gloom, she found hundreds of people lining the rails to watch the arrival of the *Albara*. The ship's outline could just be seen out on the dark sea, less than a quarter of a mile away. A man next to Ann lent her his binoculars and she was able to take a good look at the ship. Somehow she had expected a modern destroyer, with sleek lines. What she saw was squat and slightly old-fashioned.

"Not much to look at, is she?" said the owner of the binoculars. "Perhaps she's working under cover. You know, the way they do in the movies."

"Perhaps," said Ann doubtfully.

Ann returned the binoculars and the man said "Now, we'll show the beggars! We'll teach these terrorists to try it on with us?"

Ann nodded hopefully and began to search for Foxy Fanfare.

She looked along the decks, in the main lounge, the card room and both dining rooms. They certainly were proving very elusive. She also drew a blank at

111

the lido and the health spa and the gymnasium.

During her travels she came upon Frank, hopping along with a pair of crutches and a heavily bandaged leg.

"I'm not staying down there!" he told her. "If the ship went down I'd be a dead duck!"

"Is Madame Pavlova any better?" Ann asked without any real hope.

"She is, as a matter of fact," he replied. "Game old bird she is. Sitting up when I left."

"Sitting up!"

He nodded. "She's incredible. Sipping tea from one of those teacups with a spout. The doc couldn't get over it! Tickled pink, he was."

"I should think so," Ann agreed. "I really thought she was going to die."

Feeling a little more cheerful Ann began a second tour of the ship, convinced that sooner or later she would find Foxy Fanfare.

Twenty minutes later she still had not found them and the certainty was growing that their disappearance was no accident. On a sudden impulse she made her way back to the captain's cabin. To her surprise he seemed glad to see her.

"Come in Miss Burnside," he said. "I was just going to send one of my officers to look for you. I'm afraid our troubles are not over, not by a long chalk! Scotland Yard have been in touch. I'm afraid it's bad news about Bob Stuart. He was found dead in his flat. Extensive head injuries."

"They killed him? Oh no! Not Mr Stuart!"

"I'm afraid so. There were signs of a struggle and the telephone had been wrenched from the wall. Poor man. We are up against ruthless murderers."

Ann felt a rush of sympathy for the captain who suddenly looked so much older. His face had lost all its colour and his eyes were haggard. So many lives depended on him – it was an awesome burden.

For a moment she thought about the entertainments manager, a cheerful, plump young man who had done nothing to deserve such a terrible fate. Furiously she blinked back tears. "Frank Whitby should be told," she suggested. "The man who scalded his leg. He was Bob Stuart's friend."

"I've just sent him a message," the captain told her, "and I'm afraid that's not the end of the bad news, Miss Burnside. You'd better read this."

He handed her another radio message. Ann read it out loud:

"We have Foxy Fanfare Stop Release Abd el Rahman Stop Deadline midnight."

With dread in her heart Ann glanced at her watch. It was already ten minutes past ten!

Up on deck once more Ann joined in a cheer as a helicopter loomed suddenly above them and the down draught from the rotor blades blew everyone's hair. They ducked, laughing, and were running for cover when a harsh voice in the darkness boomed above the noise of the helicopter's engines.

"We have a machine gun trained on you." The

man spoke with a foreign accent. "We do not play games. The bomb was a warning. We will not hesitate to achieve our aims."

A terrible silence had fallen over the passengers who now stared upward in shocked disbelief. A man near Ann cried: "That ship can't be the *Albara*!" and a great babble of frightened comment broke out. People nearest to the doors rushed inside to the comparative safety of the corridors. Anything was better than remaining on deck beneath that menacing machine. Those that were not near enough to a door found whatever shelter they could. Some huddled below the lifeboats, others behind piles of deck chairs. Ann found herself pressed up against the wall by a number of terrified passengers who could find no better hiding place but dared not risk a run to anywhere more secure.

"Oh Jay!" she thought desperately and crossed her fingers that he at least had reached safety.

A burst of machine gun fire shattered the darkness but the bullets hissed harmlessly into the sea.

"Do as we tell you and you will not get hurt!" the voice boomed again and once more the terrified passengers fell silent, waiting and watching.

"If anyone moves you'll all get it!"

If this was not the friendly ship they had been expecting, where was the *Albara*? What had happened to Captain Spence and the military personnel that had been promised? Was no one going to help them?

Ann's thoughts were still wildly chaotic when a searchlight was switched on above them and a fierce white beam played on the ship's bridge. All faces turned in that direction and a gasp of horror burst from every throat. In the light they saw three figures being manhandled down the steps. They were gagged and their arms were bound behind them.

"Foxy Fanfare!" whispered Ann.

Now, when it was too late, she could see the connection behind the group and the bomb. The terrorists' weapon was two-pronged and Foxy Fanfare were part of it! That was where Toddy came into the plot. He must have been bribed or forced to co-operate. Presumably the bomb had detonated prematurely and had failed to cripple the ship. Now they were forced to switch plans. They were going to kidnap Foxy Fanfare! They would trade the lives of Sam, Foxy and Mick for the release of the prisoner.

Everything was falling into place in Ann's mind and she could see it all with appalling clarity. What she could not see was a way to stop them.

Suddenly there was a surge from the crowd who pressed forward angrily but a quick burst of machine gun fire effectively scattered them. One man crawled away groaning and clutching his right leg. Eager hands reached out to help him and pull him back into the shadows.

The man next to Ann said, "Those blighters mean business!"

Sick at heart, Ann could only nod.

Without knowing what she intended to do, she began to work her way carefully towards the steps that led to the bridge.

She had no idea how she could help but she could not stand by and let the bombers take her friends.

"Excuse me! Excuse me!" she muttered as she elbowed her way determinedly through the crowds which were gradually dwindling as more and more people crept to safety. Soon she was near enough to see the expression on the faces of the group. Foxy was plainly terrified; Mick looked sullen; Sam's eyes were blazing.

From the helicopter a cable descended with a harness at the end. Ann's heart was pounding. So they were going to winch the hostages up, one at a time. Once in the helicopter they would be taken to the other ship and Foxy Fanfare would be at their mercy. With enough firepower the ship would become a fortress and any chance of a rescue would be small indeed.

Ann could now see that Julio held Foxy. Alfredo was holding Sam and Toddy was holding Mick. Harry Stapley was carrying a gun and looked as though he would use it.

As Julio reached for the harness he began to drag Foxy forward. She struggled as much as she could in an effort to save herself. She fell to her knees but was roughly hauled back to her feet. "Oh, Foxy!" whispered Ann, her voice agonized.

116

One of the ship's officers raced desperately towards Julio and Foxy but a bullet from Harry Stapley's gun felled him before he could reach them.

Ann heard her own voice raised in a scream: "You vicious brute!"

Around her the passengers had mostly dispersed but she could not take her eyes from the group in the spotlight. A voice from a doorway called, "Miss Burnside! Get back here. You can't do anything! They'll kill you!"

She shook her head.

"Get back here! We want to clear the decks!"

Looking round for a weapon Ann saw a fire extinguisher and snatched it from its seating. With fumbling fingers she snapped the top free. Suddenly there was someone beside her and she recognized Frank Whitby with surprise. His expression was grim and he held one of his crutches at the ready.

"I've got to have a go at them," he told her. "For what they did to poor old Bob. I'd like to strangle the lot of them with my bare hands!"

He glanced round, puzzled. "Where has everyone gone?" he whispered. "Looks like it's just you and me."

Ann nodded, her throat dry with fear. She heard Sam cry, "Let her go!" and saw him struggling with his captor as Julio began to force Foxy into the harness. Ann leaped to her feet and ran towards them. As soon as she was within reach she pressed the plunger on the extinguisher and a cloud of white foam burst out, covering both Foxy Fanfare and the bombers. Beside her Frank hobbled forward and began to lay about him with his crutch.

"Take that!" he yelled. "And that! You've killed my best mate and I'll get you for that!"

The down draught had blown some of the foam into Ann's eyes and she could no longer see what she was doing. She kept her finger on the plunger and hoped that the bombers could not see either. There were shouts from the helicopter above them but she knew they dare not fire while they could not distinguish friend from foe.

She saw Frank grappling with Julio and one of the ship's officers ran forward and dragged Foxy to safety. The extinguisher ran dry but she snatched up the fallen crutch and swung it with all her strength against Julio's legs. With a scream he doubled up and Frank knocked him senseless with his fists.

Sam was running towards her with Harry Stapley close behind him. Suddenly, to Ann's astonishment, Toddy hurled himself forward and grappled Stapley to the ground. She heard a thud as Harry's head hit the deck then Toddy had taken her arm and Sam's.

"We've got to clear the decks!" he told them.

"But where's Mick?" cried Ann.

Toddy's answer was lost in a burst of gunfire and above them the helicopter blew up with an enormous roar. Pieces of flaming metal showered

118

onto the deck and thick smoke billowed around them.

Ann found herself on the deck with Sam while Toddy sprawled over them protectively.

Gingerly they all sat up and looked at one another. They presented a sorry picture, dishevelled and covered in wisps of foam.

Ann smiled shakily. "What on earth happened?" she asked.

Toddy said, "The *Albara* turned up. She was waiting her chance to blow the helicopter out of the sky but couldn't open fire until the passengers had dispersed."

He began to unfasten Sam's gag and Ann wrestled with the cord that bound his hands.

When he was free he caught hold of Ann and hugged her.

Just then Foxy appeared, equally unkempt and with blood trickling from a cut over her left eye.

"Ann, thank goodness you're safe!" she cried, flinging her arms round her friends. "I couldn't believe my eyes when you came charging forward!"

Mick said, "She was marvellous and so was the guy with the crutch! I've never seen anything like it!"

The next few moments were confused but happy as various people arrived to congratulate them on their miraculous escape.

"I thought we were gonners when I saw that harness," Foxy confessed.

Frank hopped up to join them and was rewarded with a kiss from Foxy which made him blush furiously.

Ann turned to Toddy. "I owe you an apology," she told him. "I thought you were one of them."

"I was," he said.

Foxy stared at him. "Toddy! How could you be one of them? I don't believe it. And why did you help us? I saw you fighting with Harry Stapley."

He rubbed a hand over his face which was tired and grey with fatigue and misery.

"They made me join them," he said. "They threatened my son. They said they'd kill him if I didn't help them. They knew where he was. They had photographs of him coming out of school."

Foxy put a hand on his arm. "Oh, poor Toddy," she said. "Then it wasn't all your fault. I'm sure the police will understand."

"We'll speak up for you," said Sam.

He shook his head. "I deserve whatever I get," he muttered. "You might have been killed. I let you down." He sighed heavily. "Some manager I've turned out to be!"

One of the ship's officers came up to them. "Thank heavens you're all safe," he told them. "The captain would like to see you all as soon as you feel up to it."

Suddenly Ann clutched his arm. "Jay!" she cried. "Do you know what's happened to my brother?"

"Don't worry. He's fine," he told her. "In fact,

he's very put out because he missed all the excitement. It seems he sneaked down to the hospital to see Madame Pavlova so he wasn't even on deck."

Ann breathed a sigh of relief.

Sam asked, "What happened to the rest of the bombers?"

"Julio is under arrest," the officer told them. "His brother is dead – killed when the helicopter blew up. Harry Stapley is in protective custody in the hospital with a broken arm. He was lucky it wasn't worse."

"And the other ship?" asked Mick. "The one we thought was the *Albara*?"

"That was the *Prince Victor* chartered by a bogus South American company. They were boarded by Captain Spence's team and the remaining crew members gave themselves up. A good job this all happened at night because the *Albara* was able to approach without being seen."

Ann held out unsteady hands. "I just can't stop trembling," she said.

Toddy said, "I'm not surprised. I'm going to take you all down to the doctor for a check up." He went on, "That cut over Foxy's eye doesn't look too smart. Then I'll give myself up."

Ann said, "It could have been worse, Toddy. You could have been killed and then your son would have lost his father."

"Who wants a father who's a jail bird!" said Toddy.

"He'll understand when he's older," Foxy consoled him.

"It's the way of the world, Toddy," Sam said gently.

Ann was awake very early next morning and she lay in bed for a while thinking over the events of the past night. The fight with the terrorists seemed years ago and it was hard to believe that Toddy was no longer with them. He had given himself up and was now under arrest. He had been taken away on the *Albara* which was on its way back to New York. Foxy Fanfare would have to find themselves a new manager when they got back to London.

Somewhere in the heart of South America Abd el Rahman would have to remain in prison to complete his sentence. In London no doubt the police were looking for Bob Stuart's killer – or killers. Hopefully, before long the entire gang would be in custody, no longer a threat to innocent people. Madame Pavlova, thank goodness, was now on the way to a complete recovery.

Ann thought of how differently things might have turned out and hoped that her father would never hear *all* the details. It would be too dreadful if he decided not to let them travel on their own in future. Unfortunately, it was bound to be in all the newspapers and when they docked in London they would be mobbed by the TV crews. Still, she would worry about that when it happened. Today she would turn all her attention to the fancy dress party. Poor Madame Pavlova would have to miss it but she and Jay could go along to the hospital to show her their costumes. Better still, they could go to ask her help with the costumes and that way the old lady would share some of the fun.

Perhaps Jay could go as a pirate – she could make him a hook out of kitchen foil . . .

She glanced at her watch and saw that it was only five past six. At ten o'clock she had arranged to meet Foxy Fanfare in the lido.

They still had half the crossing to look forward to and the treasure hunt might still go ahead. Jay would enjoy that. Then there was the pleasure of seeing Mum and Gordon again. They were all going to go pony trekking for one week of the holiday and that would be fun.

With a contented sigh Ann turned over and snuggled down into the sheets. At seven o'clock she would wake Jay and another day would begin. The best part of the voyage was still to come.

Gymnast Gilly
Series

PETER AYKROYD

Gilly Denham is a budding champion gymnast – with a taste for adventure. In this exciting series, Gilly finds herself in all sorts of mysterious and dangerous situations, while trying to maintain her reputation as one of Britain's most promising young gymnasts.

1	Gymnast Gilly the Novice	£1.95	☐
2	Gymnast Gilly the Dancer	£1.95	☐
3	Gymnast Gilly the Champ	£1.95	☐
4	Gymnast Gilly the Expert	£1.95	☐

The Star Trilogy

CAROLINE AKRILL

Not all aspiring TV actresses need to ride, but when Grace Darling lands the plum part in a new TV serial, she has to learn.

1	Make Me a Star	£1.95	☐
2	Stars Don't Cry	£1.95	☐
3	Catch a Falling Star	£1.95	☐

ARMADA

The
Silver Brumby
Series

ELYNE MITCHELL

Brumbies are the wild horses of Australia, hunted by man
to be tamed for his own use. These six stories tell of
Thowra, the Silver Brumby, and Kunama, his daughter,
Wirramirra, his son, and Baringa, his grandson.

"These Brumby books are in a class by themselves . . . the
horselover's dream" *Noel Streatfeild*

The Silver Brumby	£1.95	☐
Silver Brumby's Daughter	£1.95	☐
Silver Brumbies of the South	£1.95	☐
Silver Brumby Kingdom	£1.95	☐
Silver Brumby Whirlwind	£1.95	☐
Son of the Whirlwind	£1.95	☐

ARMADA

The Chalet School
Series

ELINOR M. BRENT-DYER

Elinor M. Brent-Dyer has written many books about life at
the famous alpine school. Follow the thrilling adventures of
Joey, Mary-Lou and all the other well-loved characters in
these delightful stories, available only in Armada.

ARMADA

Stories of Mystery and Adventure by Enid Blyton
in Armada

Mystery Series

The Rockingdown Mystery	£2.25	☐
The Rilloby Fair Mystery	£2.25	☐
The Ring O'Bells Mystery	£2.25	☐
The Rubadub Mystery	£2.25	☐
The Rat-a-Tat Mystery	£2.25	☐
The Ragamuffin Mystery	£2.25	☐

Secrets Series

The Secret Island	£2.25	☐
The Secret of Spiggy Holes	£2.25	☐
The Secret Mountain	£2.25	☐
The Secret of Killimooin	£2.25	☐
The Secret of Moon Castle	£2.25	☐

All these books are available at your local bookshop or newsagent, or can be ordered from the publisher. To order direct from the publishers just tick the title you want and fill in the form below:

Name _____

Address _____

_____

Send to: Collins Childrens Cash Sales
             PO Box 11
             Falmouth
             Cornwall
             TR10 9EN

Please enclose a cheque or postal order or debit my Visa/ Access –

Credit card no:

Expiry date:

Signature:

– to the value of the cover price plus:

UK: 60p for the first book, 25p for the second book, plus 15p per copy for each additional book ordered to a maximum charge of £1.90.

BFPO: 60p for the first book, 25p for the second book plus 15p per copy for the next 7 books, thereafter 9p per book.

Overseas and Eire: £1.25 for the first book, 75p for the second book. Thereafter 28p per book.

ARMADA